THE DESIGNATED FRIEND
DREW TAYLOR

Taylor Made Publishing

contents

To my best friends,
Kaitlyn, Aubrey, and Whitney

Trigger Warning

This book contains references to past sexual assault and drug/alcohol abuse.

What's In This Book?

If you like to fully experience a book for what it is, then skip this section

TDF is a best friends to lovers road trip rom-com. These two have been besties for a while, and well, they are finally single at the same time (hehe, let the fun begin!). This book does begin with a cheating scene (not between the MCs) as it's the catalyst for things to come, so be aware if that is triggering for you.

TDF is spice free. There are, however, plenty of kisses, attraction, and longing stares. Why? Because these two are besties who have had it bad for each other for a hot minute. They aren't strangers ogling one another weirdly. Furthermore, attraction and lustful thoughts are a natural, human thing that we battle. I seek to showcase that while also having my characters learn to take their thoughts captive.

TDF contains mention of past alcohol abuse. I love how my MMC is aware of that and is so gracious with the FMC.

TDF is spice-free and written from a Christian perspective. I am a Christian, but I do not write Christian Fiction. I seek to write characters who are flawed and sinful, yet, they recognize their need for Christ and seek forgiveness, repentance, and redemption. I wanted to read a romance where faith wasn't the main storyline, yet the characters were Christian and operated from that world-view...so I wrote it. Hadley is not a Christian in this story, but she does have a beautifully woven faith arc.

Read at your own risk. And I pray you LOVE this story. Please leave a review if you do :)

Prologue

HADLEY

T hat's right, I did the dang thing!

After collapsing on my ruffled bed, out of breath from jumping up and down while squealing like a girl at a bachelorette party, I whip my phone out to text Daniel.

Me: HAPPY 6 MONTHS...AND ONE DAY! *confetti* *kissy face*

I know, most people tend to stop celebrating at the six-month mark, but this is a milestone for me: the longest relationship in my twenty-seven years. *Take that, commitment issues.*

He doesn't respond, which I expect because he's probably fast asleep. He has a big presentation tomorrow for the new marketing campaign he's trying to land at *his* firm.

Oh yes, I'm currently dating a successful businessman who owns his own marketing firm at the mere age of thirty-one. I'm doing everything opposite of my mama—finding a good man, settling down, and tossing my commitment issues to the side. Something she could never accomplish, choosing instead to turn to the bottle, pills, and countless men. I don't know who my father is, or I'd complain about him too.

I love my mama, don't get me wrong. But she has poisoned my life one too many times. It's time for me to put my past to my side and settle down with a good, stable man. My kids will know their father.

I'm too awake with happiness to try and go back to sleep, so I check in with my best friend, Braxton Rawls. He's currently working offshore and will be coming home in a couple of days.

Me: You awake?

As soon as the message is sent, I see three dots appear.

Brax: Unfortunately.

Me: Guess what???

Brax: Chicken butt.

Me: Will you ever quit with that joke? Seriously, it's old.

I decide to FaceTime him, my fingers still shaky from sheer excitement.

He picks up on the first ring and his face fills the screen. His forest green eyes are startling, even in the low light of his room. Black hair is pushed back from his face, tousled from laying down on his pillow.

I can never get over how my best friend looks like a green-eyed version of Mutt Schitt from *Schitt's Creek*.

"Hey," he says in a sleepy voice. His eyes droop halfway shut.

"I thought you said you were up?"

"I am up."

"It looks like I woke you up." I narrow my eyes.

"You did, but that doesn't mean I'm any less up now."

"My bad, Brax. I didn't know if you were working the night shift or not."

"Nothing to be sorry for," he comments, throwing an arm under his head, yawning.

I glance away from the screen for a moment, guilty feelings brewing. I shouldn't find my best friend attractive when I am in a happy, stable relationship for once. I shouldn't love him the way I do. Yes, I love him. How do you not love someone you've known for twenty years? At times, my love for him feels romantic, but mostly, it's a deep, affectionate familial love. I know my place in his life, so that brother-sister love has to win out, which is why I'm ecstatic to finally have a good man in my life that's not Braxton.

He continues speaking after a series of yawns. "I forgot to silence my phone before crashing. What are you doing up?"

"It's my longest relationship," I squeal, tossing my head back. My feet kick at the edges of the comforter. "No one can say I'm just like my mama now."

"You've never been like your mama, Dawson," he growls. Braxton's obviously not a fan of me comparing myself to Mama, but he knows how the small town of Juniper Grove, Mississippi, talks.

"You and like three other people may be the only ones who think that," I say. "But anyways, Daniel and I have been together for six months and one day now!" Another squeal of excitement escapes. "I think he's the one."

"Just…be careful, Hadley," he drawls, then yawns. I bite my tongue to keep from making a snappy comment back. He's always there, trying to warn me. To save me.

"I'm sorry I've kept you up. I'll let you go," I say, forcing my facial features to not twist in frustration.

"Nah, I'm good." The words come out jumbled as he yawns again.

"Bye, Rawls. See you in a couple of days." I fake a smile, then click to end the call.

I toss my phone to the side like I'm tossing off Braxton's warning. He's like this with all my relationships, cautious and questioning. He never fully butts in, but he also never gives the guys I date the benefit of the doubt.

And every time he "warns" me to be careful, I start to second guess myself.

That son of a gun. Why'd he have to go and rain on my parade with those little, impactful words? *Be careful*, I mock him internally.

Instead of giving in to the negative feelings creeping into my heart, I cut my lamp light off and pull my comforter to my ears.

But sleep doesn't come.

Instead, I toss and turn, my stomach growing tight and nauseous with every moment that passes. What did I eat for dinner? Daniel and I went out to dinner at a fancy restaurant in Tupelo. I had a well-done steak, mashed potatoes, and a side salad with a glass of lemon water. Nothing out of the ordinary for my diet.

My stomach churns again, and I release a groan. I drag myself out of bed on the hunt for Pepto—or anything—that can quell my stomach. Nothing. I really need to get over the whole I-won't-take-medicine-because-my-mama's-a-druggie-thing. Crawling back into bed, I open my boutique's social media page to try and distract myself.

I answer a few messages from women interested in selling their products and then switch over to my personal account. I open Daniel's message thread simply to relive some of our conversations.

My breath hitches when those four little words rest below his name: *Active two minutes ago.* Why hasn't he responded to me? I flip over to my texts, just to make sure, and there's still nothing from him. He doesn't have his messages set to *read*, so I have no idea if he actually saw it. I send him another text, a simple heart emoji, and wait.

Minutes tick by, my stomach grows angrier, and still no text. Bad thoughts deluge my brain, thoughts of car crashes and murderers. Why is he not answering me? He *always* answers me.

My gut swells and swells, and a sinking feeling of *something's wrong* settles deep into my soul. I ring Daniel, thinking if I can just hear his voice, everything will be okay.

Voicemail.

That's it. I'm going to check on him. Make sure everything's okay. Just a little drive-by to ease my fears.

And when I find everything is fine, I'm going to murder Braxton and his stupid savior complex.

I throw on a house robe over my sleep shorts and tank, slip on my knock-off Birkenstocks, grab my keys from the entryway, and head to my car.

When I pull into his driveway ten minutes later, I notice a truck that doesn't belong to him. Maybe he has a buddy over? He was talking about how a friend of his was going through a rough breakup the other day.

A light flicks on in the house. His living room light.

I cut my car off and take gentle steps until I'm by the window. My heart decides it's a racehorse trying to win the Kentucky Derby.

I stand on my tiptoes to peer into the lighted room like the creeper I'm not afraid to admit I am.

Then I lose my freaking mind.

Chapter One

Braxton

I want nothing more than to strip my clothes off and fall into bed.

It's always like this coming off a month hitch on the rig. Sleeping is the only activity I think I'm capable of doing right now, but I have to make it home before I can disappear into the sheets of my glorious bed. Two RedBulls and a cup of coffee didn't do much for me this go-round. *Almost home,* I think to myself.

I finally pull into my driveway and stumble out of my truck. Anyone looking may think I'm drunk. My log cabin home is tucked in the woods, but I do have a couple of elderly neighbors that can be seen from my front porch. I make it to the front door and fumble with the keys, trying to figure out which of the two locks I see is the right one.

My phone buzzes in my back pocket, and I don't have to take it out to know who it is. The device vibrates to the beat of "Backwoods Barbie" by Dolly Parton. She set it two years ago after she went through yet another hard breakup when I didn't answer the call on her first try. Hence the special ringtone so I always know it's her calling and can pick up.

And I'll pick up.

Every time.

Because she's my best friend, and I'll always be there for Hadley Dawson. Even if I am a zombie from *The Walking Dead*.

"Braxton! Did you make it home?" she asks as soon as I answer the phone. Her breathy voice sends shivers down my spine. I've learned to control the reaction, for the most part. But I'm dead tired and have lost my will to restrain myself.

"Hey." I clear my throat. It's scratchy like when I first wake up in the morning. Must have been the energy drinks. That six-hour drive from the port back to Juniper Grove, Mississippi, was a doozy. "Walking into my house now, Bully," I say, using the childhood nickname I gave her because she has the attitude of a feisty female bulldog. She was rightfully offended the first time I said it. But now, I think she secretly likes it. At the very least, she no longer scowls and attempts to beat me up when I use it.

"Oh, you probably want to go to sleep," she begins. The typical argument goes like this—she'll apologize for calling at ten o'clock at night. I'll tell her it's okay because I'll be up for a while anyway (even though that's not true). Hadley will make a second attempt to apologize by asking, "Are you sure?" and then I'll say, "I'm sure." We will stay on the phone for an hour, maybe two, while she tells me everything that happened while I was gone for the month as if she hadn't been texting and calling me the entire time I was on the hitch.

I don't mind it.

Because I'm in love with her.

I'm a fool who is completely enamored by his complicated, unavailable best friend.

The conversation goes as expected, though I can't help but feel like she is holding something back from me by the way she's being extra sweet. Hadley, though one of the kindest, most generous people I know, likes to let her fighter side out with me. When she's sweet, I get suspicious, but I was too tired to pry tonight. We hang up after only twenty minutes this time. I wish I can say that I drifted off into sleep, but the reality?

I dive straight into dreamland where Hadley looks at me less as her loyal dog-like best friend and more like her Fabio-esque lover. A place where her kisses bring me to my knees in worship to God for the creation in front of me.

People say a man and woman can't be best friends without wanting more...

They're right.

● ✌ ✌

The cup of black coffee warms my soul and brings light back to my eyes after sleeping in after a long night. It's eleven in the morning, and I woke up an hour ago to someone banging on my front door. My dad, Braxton Lane Rawls Sr., the notorious door-banger, sits across from me sipping on his own black coffee. I reflect on the similarities between Dad and me. We both sport dark, thick hair, though his has thinned and has the salt and pepper look now. He keeps a trimmed beard covering his cheeks and lips, as do I when I'm off the rig. We even sit the same way—leaned back in our respective chairs, legs splayed out. My height and body build come from him, but my lips, ears, and facial structure belong to my mom. A pinch of sadness always pricks me when I look in the mirror and see her features staring back. It's been two grief-filled years of not having her around. Cancer takes even the good ones.

"Well, son. How was your hitch?" Dad asks, one dark eyebrow raising as his green eyes search mine. I inwardly groan because I know exactly where this is going. He has been on me since Mom died to get a job that will keep me home more. One that doesn't take me out on the ocean for a month at a time. One that secures my safety...in his mind.

"Hard work as always," I state.

"You know, you could do well in a job that keeps you home. Maybe an office job. Or a political career. You've got the brains for it." I don't argue anymore. I sit back in my chair, prepared to deliver the usual line.

"I know, Dad. But I like hands-on work. You and Mom taught me that. And it pays well." Not a whole lie. It does pay well, and I enjoy hands-on work. But I don't enjoy offshore life per se. I would go madder than a hatter if I was stuck in an office all day, and though I stay tuned into politics, I would never throw myself into the lion's den of the political arena.

"I'm just saying, son." He throws his hands up in defense. "Look, Patton Harrison told me the other day that NAVO was hiring for—"

"Dad," I warn, giving him the look that says *you-won't-win-this.* When will he realize this is my life and not his? "I don't want a desk job in the oceanographic field."

"What about taking Michael up on his offer to join his construction company?" I think back to my brother-in-law's offer prior to this month's hitch. Honestly, it was enticing. He would hire me to be the architect of a line of log houses, similar to my own. I would have to go back to school for a degree though. I'm not opposed to school. I'm actually an avid learner, but it wouldn't be feasible to go back to school at the age of twenty-nine. I'll be thirty in a few months, so I need to remain settled... Stick to life's current direction.

I sigh, letting my head fall toward my chest before answering Dad. "I'm happy where I'm at." Again, not a full lie, but just enough to get him off my case for now.

"Just be safe out there, son." He shakes his head once, picking up his black coffee for another sip. I join him and redirect the conversation to Thursday Night Football while we make bets on the final score of the game tonight. The New Orleans Saints have it in the bag against Detroit.

While talking about past games, my phone buzzes with Hadley's text pattern. It's a series of vibrations in quick three-toned beats. I have no idea what it is supposed to be, but when it comes to Hadley Dawson, it's easier to just roll with things.

Bully: Wanna watch the game tonight at my place?

Me: Dad is over. My place?

Bully: Sure. I'll make that limeade punch you like!

Me: Great. I got the *taco emoji* stuff

Bully: *zany face emoji*

Me: *winky face*

"Who's making you grin like that?" Good ole Dad. Always on the hunt to wife me up.

"It's just Hadley. She's coming over for the game."

"*Just* Hadley?" It's one of those statements that you know is actually a question.

"Yes, *just* Hadley," I emphasize back. It's not just him. I can't go anywhere in this little community of Juniper Grove without someone bringing Hadley Dawson up like we are a couple. When will they learn that we are *just* friends?

I look down at my phone and watch as three dots appear and disappear three times over.

When will I learn?

Chapter Two

HADLEY

T he thrum of country chic music floats through the boutique.

My boutique, I smile to myself, wiggling my shoulders and flipping my hair.

Southern Grace Boutique and Gift Market has been open for three years now, coming on the heels of my region-wide jewelry company, Tease Jewelry, that I started five years ago.

And they say women who have alcohol-addicted mamas, who don't know who their father is, and who have practically raised themselves with the assistance of grandmamas can't be successful in life.

At least I still have this place and my company, I sigh. Lying and cheating ex-boyfriends come and go, but my company shall reign forever!

"Morning, boss." Karoline Wright bounces through the front doors. Karoline is my college student employee who not only keeps this place on trend with social media but also pulls in all of her college friends.

"Coffee?" I ask, gesturing to my office in the back which hosts a simple coffee pot.

"You know I'm a tea kind of girl." She laughs, holding up her cup from Books and Beans, the local coffee shop that has a quaint bookstore attached to it. "So, what's the plan while you're away for the next ten days?"

"Don't remind me." I groan, remembering the road trip to Mary Anne's wedding in Virginia I had planned.

With Cheater Daniel.

Who is no longer my boyfriend as of three days ago.

I let Karoline in on that piece of information.

"I'm going to cut his—"

"Whoa, girl." I throw my hands up in laughter, then wink. "Beat you to it." Her jaw drops, but she catches my tease and shakes her head.

"Men." She spits the word like it's the nastiest of curses while her fists clench at her side. Before I can ask her what's wrong, she relaxes and her face softens. "How are you?"

"I'm—" I don't really know. I've never been cheated on before. Dumped? Yes, though rarely. But I've never caught my boyfriend in the act of cheating. I shove the image of the tall redhead who clung to his body like a leech from my mind. "I'll be okay." It's the best I got right now. I'm trying to forget that Daniel ever happened. Tacos and the football game with Braxton and his dad last night helped to redirect my mood for a moment, but then the venom-loaded feelings came back as I lay in my bed and cried myself to sleep last night.

"Are you still going to Mary Anne's wedding?"

"Yes ma'am, that's the plan," I say, trying my best to perk up from the sour thoughts.

"So, who are you leaving in charge?" she questions.

"You, duh," I state. Shouldn't she know this already? Karoline is top of her class at Juniper Grove University, the number one private school in the state of Mississippi. I'm still reeling over the fact she chose to work for my little business. She's quickly become my right-hand woman since Mary Anne moved to Virginia a couple of months ago. I wouldn't choose any of my other employees to run the store over Karoline.

"But what about when I have class? I can't be here until two in the afternoon each day." Oh, yeah. I sometimes forget that college students still have to go to classes. Karoline is not my personal magic elf who can be available at any given moment, though I sometimes feel like she is.

"I'll have Jane and Candace alternate openings. Do you want to alternate closing with anyone?" I do trust all my employees or else they wouldn't be here. But there's something special about Karoline.

"Nah, I'm good to close each night. As long as you still let me do my homework." *Thank goodness!*

"Of course." I grin. "As long as you keep the store's social media account growing and bringing in customers!" I've got to keep *something* steady in my life now since a man obviously isn't going to be that.

"Easy as cake." She feigns blowing me a kiss before walking into the front of the store. I often forget the woman is twenty-one, a whole six years younger than me, because her maturity level and work ethic are off the charts.

"Oh, and Karoline," I holler after her. I hear her heels clicking as she walks back to my little office tucked here in the back of the store. She pokes her head in.

"Yes?"

"Thank you for everything you do. I couldn't run this place without you. Especially now that Mary Anne went and moved on us. Southern Grace Boutique needs you, Tease Jewelry needs you, and I need you. Expect an exceptional bonus this coming Christmas."

"I'm here as long as you'll keep me," she says. "You've taught me so much that school could never teach. You're the best boss!"

"I want a mug that proves it," I jest. "Don't forget I'm leaving at noon today." She salutes me, then clicks off towards the front. The girl is odd, but a boutique genius.

My phone buzzes. I pick it up to see the local jail as the caller.

Mama.

Maybe it's not her. I haven't seen her in a few weeks, but I never know when she will land herself in jail again.

I don't need any more bad news.

W hat's one more gallon of spoiled milk to add to the one you already have?

I keep my eyes on the two-lane street as I dig in my purse for a lollipop. The road rumbles beneath my tires as I drive home in silence, contemplating what the best course of action is. If Grandmama were here, she'd tell me to leave my mama's butt in jail. She'd tell me if I kept bailing her out, my mama would never learn her lesson. If I bailed her out this time, it would be the third time in the span of eight months.

Rose Lynn Dawson is the World's Worst Mom, but I love her.

Because she's my mama.

What is it Braxton always says? If you truly love someone, you have to help them see the truth? I don't like the idea of Mama spending time in jail. I don't even know what she's in for this time. Probably alcohol or drug-related.

Maybe she needs to stay locked up a little while this time. I don't have time to deal with all the complications anyways. I need to pack and get ready to leave tomorrow. She can wait until the road trip is over, and maybe a little time in the slammer for once will do her some good.

So it's settled.

I push her out of my mind as I pull into my driveway, get out of my car, and make my way to the front door. The strawberry lollipop in my mouth gives me a small boost of joy in the midst of the sour lemons of life. I dig in my purse for my keys.

After finding my keys buried at the bottom of my purse under layers of old receipts, lollipops, and half-used chapsticks, I let myself into the little cottage house my grandmama left me in her will when she passed away two years ago.

Shoot, I left the music on again.

Carrie Underwood sings about cheaters, tire slashing, and fruity drinks through Grandmama's vintage speakers. Like I needed the reminder...

My phone buzzes in three repetitive vibrations in my pocket as I cut the music off. Braxton. I set the same text pattern on his phone, though he'll never figure out what it means. My day brightens instantly as I pick the phone out of my back pocket.

Brax: You home yet? Movie night?

"Someone's bored," I chuckle aloud to myself. We had so much fun yesterday watching the game and eating tacos. It really helped me to take my mind off of Cheater Daniel. Braxton's company always spearheads a sense of joy in my life.

Geez, I've got to wipe the stupid grin off my face. Even though I'm now single, I CANNOT be smiling at the thought of my best friend.

Why?

Here's a list:

1. He's my best friend.

2. He knew me in middle school (cringe).

3. I was just cheated on after celebrating my longest relationship.

4. He works offshore.

5. My abandonment, trust, and reinforced commitment issues won't allow me to date anyone who can't see me for a whole month at a time.

See? Braxton and I would NEVER work. And I can't risk trying on the slim hope he may like me as more than a friend because if it crashes and burns like my past experiences, then I lose my best friend. Blame it on the daddy issues. Or lack-of-daddy issues.

I do.

But now I'm in a predicament.

I'm dateless for Mary Anne's wedding next Saturday in Virginia. The road trip I had planned for Daniel and me was epic if I do say so myself. I hate planning things, but I planned this for us because I was naive and "sure" that he just might have been the one. *Stupid, stupid girl.*

And it wasn't just any road trip, but a Hallmark movie-level romantic one.

Mary Anne is—well, was—my second in command at the boutique and is one of my closest friends. She helped me build my brand from the ground up, and I know she would never judge me. But others from this neck of the woods? They always judge. ALWAYS. No matter how many career milestones I reach—like being a total boss babe. It's nothing compared to the holy union of marriage according to southern women. A woman's success is tied to marriage. No matter if it's a healthy and happy one. You got a ring on your finger? Well, honey...you've won at this game of life.

Moral of the story: one doesn't show up alone to a southern wedding.

And I have to go because I am a bridesmaid. A person can't just bail out of being a bridesmaid.

Which means I have to ask one of my ridiculous exes to accompany me on a romantic getaway to Chesapeake, Virginia. Daniel sure as heck ain't coming now.

Or...

I can ask my best friend who I'm extremely attracted to on a romantic getaway to a wedding and pray to the God I'm not sure exists that he will say yes.

Braxton? An ex?

The decision is easy.

My fingers fly over my phone as I text Braxton back, letting him know to come over for dinner. I'll feed him, then coerce him.

I crunch the rest of my lollipop down, then grab the things I need to whip up a pot of spaghetti out of my pantry. After turning on my Dolly Parton record using Grandmama's turntable, I get to cooking.

● ✌ ☝

Turns out I felt like making garlic bread and baking homemade cookies to go with our spaghetti.

"Are you sure this is a good idea?" Lorelei Spence, one of my female best friends, has spent the past thirty minutes on a video call with me while I cooked after I texted to let her know I would be asking Braxton to accompany me to Virginia for the wedding. "Maybe *you* need a getaway by *yourself* for a change. Collect yourself. Discover who you are without a man."

Lorelei and her twin sister, Lucy, came to my rescue a few nights ago after I lost my good graces on Daniel. I shudder, recalling the monster I morphed into. There were a lot of curses, physical objects were thrown, and glass splinters littered his living room floor. The girls came over, calmed me down, and fed me ice cream while we watched *Stranger Things*. Nothing like a good suspenseful, horror, sci-fi show to get your mind off things.

"It'll practically be like I'm alone," I retort, forcing myself back into the present. I've got to quit reliving that night. "It's Braxton."

"It's about time she goes for that. I was contemplating it if she didn't," Lucy exclaims behind her.

"He's not a piece of meat. You can't just refer to him as 'that'." Lorelei shoves her sister back. They look identical with curly strawberry blonde hair, soft hazel eyes, and splatters of freckles across their noses and cheeks. But I know that Lorelei has a brown birthmark on her left cheek much like Marilyn Monroe. If she covers it, the two sisters merge into one.

"Ladies, chill," I interrupt, taking the cookies out of the oven. "I'm not gunning for him. I just got out of a relationship with a two-timing scumbag. And anyways, Brax and I are *just friends.*" I feel like I've been emphasizing that more than usual lately. As kids, and then youth, Braxton and I were always told by our elders that we would end up marrying. But as we grew older, our relationship grew into a tight bond like a brother and sister would have. Into our twenties, people generally left us alone because either he'd have a girlfriend or I'd have a boyfriend. But then there were rare moments like this one where we were single at the same time and all the romantic feelings and fantasies I've had—and often repressed—roared to life.

"Friends-to-lovers is a popular romance trope for a reason." Lucy winks. The woman practically lives in romance novels when she's not trying to write her own. "Maybe you'll live out your own."

I elevate my voice and speak clearly, enunciating each word. "JUST. FRIENDS. No lovers part."

"Whatever you say, Hads," they say at the same time. Good gracious, I hate when they do that. And since when did Lorelei jump to Team Braxton & Hadley? I glare at her.

"How's Jake doing?" One mention of Lucy's boyfriend will deter any more comments on my love life with Braxton.

Not that I have a love life with Braxton.

"He's taking me out to dinner tonight at *La Bella*." Lucy grabs the phone from her sister. "I think he might propose." *Le sigh.* Here we go. Lucy is always on the hunt for her husband. She complains that writing romance isn't satisfying her itch, so she's been falling in love with every guy that shows her interest lately. She gets too emotionally involved and scares them away, but I don't know how to tell her to stop. I don't want to curb her appetite for love...even if I don't quite understand her intense desires.

"It's only been three months." Lorelei gapes at her twin.

"I'm with her." I smirk, nodding towards Lorelei. I had finally made it to six months and was just beginning to entertain the idea of him being the one. At least this time it wasn't a breakup of my own accord. His cheating did that. No one can say I'm like my mama when breaking up wasn't something I chose, right?

"But I know he's the one. He must feel it too." Her eyes become dream clouds. Lucy's always been the hopeless romantic, a swoony-whimsical queen. Lorelei is the strategic, head-on-straight, mama hen. Me? I just try to keep my head above water most days. Especially the past couple of days.

Lorelei and I spend the next twenty minutes trying to talk Lucy off her romance high so she won't have her hopes up for dinner with Jake. My doorbell rings, and I tell the girls I've got to go.

After we click off, Lorelei sends me a private message.

Lor-a-Lie: You deserve goodness, Hads.

I pause for a moment, fighting back the tears threatening to smudge my expertly crafted makeup. The doorbell rings again.

"Coming," I shout while typing a response back to Lorelei.

Me: I luv you.

Lor-a-Lie: I luv you, too.

I open the door and meet the bright eyes of my best friend. The one who instantly makes me feel like all is right in the world. He walks in and makes himself at home.

Another text comes through, this one from Lucy.

Luce Goose: Keep your location on. *winky face* *kissy face* *hug*

Me: You think Brax will murder me? *eye roll*

Luce Goose: Course not. Just do it. For me. *praying hands* *kissy face*

Me: *thumbs up* *eye roll*

My phone vibrates with an incoming call from DO NOT ANSWER—the new name the local jail sports on my phone as a reminder.

I don't.

Chapter Three

Braxton

"It smells like Italy in here." I sniff the air, always impressed with Hadley's cooking. "With a side of good ole chocolate chip cookies. And Dolly Parton."

"Have you ever been to Italy?" Her voice is sardonic as she tucks her phone into her back pocket. She knows I haven't. We've been glued at the hip since she was seven and I was nine, besides those few years of college.

Releasing a tired groan, I pull the lever on the side of the couch and let the footrest pop out. Dolly sings about Jolene, and I half expect to hear Hadley screaming-singing the lyrics. Instead, she rushes to the turntable and cuts it off.

"I thought you loved that song," I comment. She looks at me with a pained expression before whipping around and heading toward the kitchen.

I fight my way out of the old sinking couch cushion and follow her. She looks like she might cry at any given moment.

"Hads, what's wrong?" I ask, rounding the corner. Her hands are splayed on the kitchen counter, her face covered by long, shiny platinum hair. She sniffles, and I walk to her side. Placing a hand on her back, I ask again. "What's wrong, Hadley?"

"He, Dan—" she stutters on the name before sniffling again, "cheated on me."

My blood boils under my skin, and I'm pretty sure this is what people mean when they say they are seeing red.

"Daniel cheated on you?" I ask again, making sure I heard her right. She nods her head before turning to me. I wrap her in my arms, squeezing her tight. A sweet, floral scent that only belongs to Hadley infiltrates my senses as I bury my face into her hair. "That no-good, low-life, son of a gun. I could kill him."

"I almost did." She laughs between sobs. "I slapped him real hard. The girl he was with had no clue about what to—"

"You caught him with a girl?!" Outrage consumes me. She WITNESSED him cheating?

"You're holding me too tight," Hadley says in breaths. I relax my grip, but don't let her go.

"Since you didn't kill him, I'll take the torch up and do it," I bite. She pulls away and looks up at me with black, tear-stained cheeks. I swear, I'll rip that idiot's face off for what he's done to my best friend. To my Hadley.

"I don't need you to do anything, Braxton." She pokes a finger into my chest. "I took care of it myself. And regardless of my current *situation*..." she sweeps a hand toward her face, "I really am okay." She wipes at the black smudges beneath her eyes, but nothing comes away. Ignoring her little rant, I rip a paper towel from the holder, dab it in water from the sink, and cup her face with my free hand. Glacier blue eyes stare into mine as I gently wipe at the coal-colored blotches beneath her eyes and down her cheek. I have no clue what I'm doing, but this seemed like the appropriate course of action. Except nothing is coming off her face.

"Is this stuff waterproof or just me proof?"

She laughs, and it's the most inviting sound I've ever heard. "Yes, it is waterproof actually."

"No wonder I can't get it off." Her eyes grow wide for a moment before she turns her face away from me.

"It's okay. Like I said, I don't need your help. Let me freshen up in the bathroom." She swats the air. "Go ahead and fix yourself a plate."

I watch her walk away, wondering if I should follow, before deciding to stay. I turn to the food, grab a plate off the countertop, and pile it high with noodles and spaghetti sauce. The fantastic woman even made meatballs! I stick five on my plate before taking my food and sitting back down on the couch. I'm not much of a couch-eater, but Hadley is. And she's the one who needs comfort tonight.

Shoving a huge bite into my mouth, I start to contemplate different ways to confront Daniel because there is no way he is going unconfronted by me. Cheating is *not* okay. I know his address, and his face is calling my fist.

"Want to watch a Marvel movie or something?" Hadley walks into the living room, all the black from under her eyes gone. It looks like she put on more makeup for that matter, like she was never crying.

"Cool with *Iron Man*?"

"Go ahead and put it on while I make my plate," she says, disappearing into the kitchen. Why yes ma'am, I will.

"What's with you cooking this delicious meal and playing my favorite movie?" I stuff another meatball into my mouth. Sweet heavens, this is good. "I should be the one cooking you a meal. And wouldn't you rather watch *Twilight* or something?" I want to kick myself for even suggesting the ridiculous movie, but I refrain. Whatever Hadley wants tonight, I will bend to her will.

"Just trying to take my mind off things," she responds from the kitchen. "No romantic movies tonight. Besides, you'd cook something healthy that would probably kill my carb-loaded body." Ignoring her jab at my eating habits, I continue to think of what I want to do to Daniel. I think I'll pay him a visit when I leave tonight, but right now, Hadley needs me here.

"Well, hurry up and let's get started on the whole taking your mind off things," I holler back, trying not to spit meatball out of my mouth. She walks out of the kitchen with her own plate, while holding two glasses of sweet tea. Can this woman get any better? I take a glass from her, drink a swig, then hit play on the movie that I pulled up on her streaming account while she made her plate.

For the record, I'm pretty sure this is as close to Heaven as Earth can get.

Hadley sits down beside me. Not on the other cushion, but in the couch crevice. Her legs are smushed up against mine, making it a little hard to breathe.

And that's when it hits me: Hadley and I are single at the same time. I know she's upset, but hey, I've always been the shoulder she's cried on or the guy who's there when no one else is. I can be that person one more time, but then... I want more. I just have to make my move before another guy swoops in like they have in the past.

This time, my best friend is not slipping through my fingertips.

Hadley

"Please, Brax." I flash my soft baby blues at him and bat my black, thickly mascaraed eyelashes. For extra measure, I reach out and gently brush his forearm before grabbing his hand. Do I notice the rippled muscles beneath his suntanned skin?

Of course I do.

How can one have rippled forearm muscles?

Ask Braxton Rawls.

"I can't up and leave for Virginia tomorrow morning." He shifts his eyes to my hand on his arm and his tone to something more of a question than a statement. Aw, come on! I fed the guy AND let him watch his favorite movie. I was hoping I'd buttered him up enough tonight.

"It'll be an adventure! You've always talked about how you'd like to see more of the country. Virginia is a good place to start." His eyebrows raise in contemplation. Is he truly considering this? I know it's asking a lot of my best friend, but he has always been there. When I needed a date to the middle school Winter Nights dance—Braxton. A shoulder to cry on when Mama got to be too much? Braxton. Someone to laugh with and indulge my childish behaviors with as a grown adult? I'd call Braxton. He's always been down for a mud fight in the middle of a summer rainstorm.

He's never said no before. In fact, I think he likes being there for me, even if it's only like an older brother. This better not be the time he starts saying no.

"I don't know, Dawson..." he begins, but I cut him off again. I let my hand fall from his arm and place it into the back pocket of my ripped, faded high-waisted mom jeans.

"Listen, Rawls. It'll be six days on the road there with some pretty fun activities. We will be participating in wedding festivities for two days, then traveling home for two. That's ten days total. You'll still have time to rest or do whatever it is you want to do before going back offshore." I know, *I know.* I'm asking so much from him. He typically uses his month off to decompress and work on the home he has been building for himself. But I'm too desperate to let this go without a well-given fight on my end. If Mama taught me one thing, it was how to use my feminine charm on a man. I don't like to be manipulative, but desperate times call for desperate measures.

Besides, flirting with Braxton is nothing new to me. Teasing him is my favorite pastime.

I tilt my head to the side, pouting my bottom lip ever so slightly. I let my eyes grow a little wider, blinking a few more times. Dilated eyes are apparently one of the most attractive qualities in a person. It shows affection and interest.

He thinks for a moment longer, his dark green eyes searching mine. They dilate as he continues to study me. What's going on in that big brain of his?

"I need you, Braxton." I play my damsel in distress card, hoping it triggers that savior complex of his. But he only continues to stare with mild amusement. "Fight for it?" I suggest, resorting to my last-ditch effort.

His lips tug upward for a brief moment and he nods. We take our stances.

"Rock, paper, scissors, shoot!" we yell in unison. I pull scissors, as I always do on my first round. He pulls rock, which is to be expected.

"Rock, paper, scissors, shoot!"

He shocks me by pulling paper, whereas he typically pulls rock. He covers my hand, still sitting in the rock position, with his hand—calloused, working hands on top of smooth, porcelain skin. My shoulders sink, and I feel my cheeks redden a bit. *He must really not want to go with me to win out in the second round.* It'd be pointless to deny that we know each other's moves by heart in this little game we play.

"Fine, I'll go." He suppresses a smile, but I see it trying to break through. My heart swells at this kind, albeit testing, man. "But you owe me a gazillion coffees, some of that lemon hand soap from your store, and several homemade delicious meals you conjure up."

"Your wish is my command," I say, bowing my head and rubbing my hands together to give full-on genie vibes. Thank goodness he said yes.

"Such a weirdo." He shakes his head and laughs. That carefree sound sends me to Cloud Nine. In fact, Braxton is the sole pilot that can get me there these days.

"You sure we can't just fly?" he asks. "Then we could just spend a week touring historical sights in Virginia."

"Not a chance, Rawls. I planned an epic trip." I grab his hand again, intertwining his calloused fingers between my dainty ones. "And if you rub me the right way on the road trip you may get more wishes and favors."

I watch his face turn shade after shade of red. I expect him to push away and change the subject like he typically does when I try a little flirting out on him. But instead, he grasps my hand tighter, leans down so that our faces are mere inches from each other, and whispers, "You're on."

I'm a girl who doesn't blush. So I'm positive the heat flooding my face is in no way manifesting itself as a color.

I think.

That's not the typical "older brother" type of action I've come to expect from him. What alien took over my best friend's mind to make *him* say something like *that* to *me*?

CHAPTER FOUR

BRAXTON

The designated friend. That's all I've ever been to Hadley, and now I have to figure out how to change that label. It has to happen smoothly and in increments so I don't push her away.

When she asked me yesterday to accompany her on the road trip to a wedding in Virginia, a million red flags shot up. *Abort, Abort,* my mind screamed, much like my older sister Brandi sounded when I told her on the phone what my plan was. I needed to make sure Dad was looked after while I was away. Much like my month-on, month-off job, Brandi and I take turns checking on Dad.

But I've been at my breaking point lately when it comes to Hadley, and I've almost told her how much I love her on more than one occasion. I don't know when I realized I loved her. Maybe it was the moment I watched her invite a girl who was eating lunch by herself to sit with us in the cafeteria in high school? Or maybe it was after all the times I consoled her when she broke down under the stress of caring for her alcohol and drug-addicted mother. Heck, it was probably all the times she's given me her cheeky smile...her true smile. Not the fake one she puts on for the rest of society. There are too many moments to note that could have been the turning point from mere friend to romantic interest.

After my mom's death, it felt extra important to hold Hadley close, which meant spending even more time with her and falling deeper in love with the woman who would seemingly never be mine in the way I so desperately craved.

All while she dated man after man, ending with that douche, Daniel.

I clench and unclench my fist, my knuckles still feeling a little sore from that one punch. Daniel didn't see it coming last night. I knocked on his door, he opened it, and I put the entirety of my muscle mass and size behind one blazing punch of glory. He fell down, I might have spit on him (not too proud, but maybe just a little), and told him he never deserved a woman like Hadley.

She doesn't know any of this, and I plan to keep it that way. She said she handled him herself, and I believe it from what she told me last night while we watched the movie. But I couldn't *not* step in.

She's my best friend. The woman I'm in love with.

Now I'll be spending ten days with her in my truck, at a wedding, and in whatever sleeping arrangements she has? *Take me now, Lord,* I pray. *Because if You don't, she will.* I want to respect that she just got out of a relationship that hurt her, but I've been waiting for this moment for *so long*.

I don't believe in soulmates, but I do believe in God. He knew I'd need Hadley more times than I care to admit throughout my life. He knew she would need me. And dang it...why can't we just be a couple? Why can't she see me the way I see her?

No, I don't believe in soulmates, but I do believe in choosing one person day after day.

And I've been choosing Hadley since I was nine years old.

It's time she knows how I feel. I'm tired of being king of the friend zone and an older brother to her. I'm tired of hiding my feelings for her. Hence why I took her flirty challenge head-on yesterday. She's not getting away with low-level flirting with me just to make me give in to her anymore. Nope. She wants to flirt? Fine. I've dated around. I was quite notorious for it in my high school and early college years. I know how to flirt, and I know exactly what buttons to push when it comes to her... What makes her tick.

So here I stand on my front porch with a large suitcase packed full, a duffle bag, and my laptop bag. I'm wickedly smiling to myself, thinking of all the ways I plan to make my best friend fall head over heels for me in the next ten days.

"Where ya goin'?" Still grinning to myself, I turn my head towards my neighbor, Hank Jones, who is sitting on his front porch swing. A twinge of sadness appears at the sight of his log cabin home. I helped Mom build it with her team a few years after we moved to the area.

"To Virginia," I shout back, knowing the old man is hard of hearing. The distance between our houses doesn't help.

"Why you goin' to Virginia?"

"To finally get the girl," I holler. All the men around the world beat their chests in solidarity with my decision.

"A girl in Virginia?" His confounded voice trickles across the lawn.

"The girl a little ways down the road." My heart swells, and I hope this mustered confidence doesn't disappear later. He continues to stare at me like I've lost it, then shakes his head and goes back to sipping his coffee.

Five in the morning is his usual time to front-porch-sit, definitely not mine when I am home. But I'm up, energetic, and ready to go.

I'm going to get the girl who grew up three minutes down the road from my family home, and I'm going to get her by going to Virginia.

I pull up to Hadley's small brick house, much different than the cabin-style wooded home I'm continually working on for myself. Hadley's home is full of pastel colors and country chic (as she calls it) decor. Mine will be decorated with deep tones of brown, green, and blue. Tones of the earth. Earth chic? Is that a thing?

She has several potted ferns hanging from her front porch with daisy wind chimes playing a soft tune in the gentle morning breeze. A song of hope, of possibilities to come.

I leave my truck running, hop out, and knock on her door.

No answer.

I knock again to no avail. *If this woman is still sleeping...*

Rummaging behind her white porch chair with frilly pink cushions, I reach for the hide-a-key rock, take the key out, and unlock the door.

The house is still dark and quiet. I flip on the living room light and make my way down the small hallway to her room, frustration building. Her door is open, and I find her snoozing away, laying on her side facing me. I walk a little closer, though I know I should probably turn the light on and make my presence known. She's usually a light sleeper, but the roaring fan in her room must tune out all other noise.

How can I be angry though? She's so darn cute when she sleeps. How could Daniel choose anyone over this angel? Watching her sleep sucks the frustration right out of me. Her platinum hair is frizzy and fanned out on her pillow, giving me a complete view of her full face and plump lips. I reach out my hand towards her without thought. I need to feel those lips beneath my thumb...

Her eyes fly open, the typically crystal blue color a menacing black in the darkness of the room. Hadley flings herself across the bed away from me and falls on the floor. I stifle a laugh and flick on her light.

Hadley Dawson is an easy target! Just thought I'd let all the murderers out there know.

She pokes her head above the bed, her hair halfway in front of her face. I watch as her body decompresses in relief.

"What the heck, Rawls? You scared the mess out of me." She clutches her chest and stands up. I quickly look away because only an oversized t-shirt covers her body.

But wait...

"That's my t-shirt." I whip my head back around, staring at my old Nirvana shirt that I wore during my rock phase in college. My heart picks up a beat.

Holy cow.

What is she doing sleeping in one of *my* t-shirts?

A blush fills her face, and to be quite frank, I don't believe I've ever seen her blush before. Well, other than yesterday when I decided to flirt back with her.

But I haven't seen her without makeup in a ridiculously long time.

And let me tell you, boys... She's beautiful.

Hadley grabs a blanket off her bed and covers herself up, letting her hair completely shield her face as she plops down on the bed.

"Get out!" she shouts at me, but I can't help but stand there and think of the beautiful woman—her pale skin, platinum hair, and icy blue eyes. A woman who's so full of light but thinks she is messed up beyond repair.

"Rawls! Out!" I come to my senses and realize this is a *perfect* opportunity.

"It's—" I glance at the digital clock on her nightstand, "5:34 in the morning. You were supposed to be ready by 5:30, Bully." I sit down next to her, reaching my hand out to tuck her hair from her face. She swats my hand away before I get the chance to touch her.

"I'll be ready in ten minutes." She clears her throat while looking away, trying to hide her face. "Just get out, okay?" I watch her shoulders slump, and I do what she asks because the uneasiness and hurt lacing her voice cuts me deep. Why is she hiding her face? Because she isn't wearing makeup?

It had never dawned on me until that moment that I had never seen Hadley without makeup. Not once since middle school, at least.

Was that causing her uneasiness?

I backtrack outside to shut my truck off, then I turn on her television, brew a pot of coffee, and fry Hadley a few eggs.

Ready in ten minutes, my butt, I scoff, knowing good and well we are going to be over an hour late heading out on the road trip *she* planned.

Just roll with it, I remind myself. *No sense in getting tight-wadded over a road trip schedule that you didn't plan.*

I slump into the couch when my phone rings. My sister.

"Hello?" I answer.

"Hey, Bratz, what's up?" she asks, using the nickname she gave me when I was born. According to our parents, it's because she couldn't fully say my name at her young age of three.

"Waiting on Hadley to finish getting ready before we leave."

She sighs. "Are you sure about this?" This is not the first time she has asked me this question. And to be honest, I'm kind of getting tired of it.

"I'm a grown man, Brandi. I can manage my own affairs. Er, I mean road trips." This is NOT an affair with Hadley. Just a road trip with my best friend. At least, that is what I keep telling everyone. No one knows my plans to make Hadley mine. No one but my neighbor Ole Hank Jones, that is.

"You've had googly-eyes for that woman since we moved to Juniper Grove. And you're always at her beck and call, swooping in to help her."

"So what?" I ball my fist at my side. "So what if I want to be there for her? No one else is. Why can't I date her? That would be *my* business and not yours." I check my surroundings, making sure Hadley hasn't stepped outside her room for some reason. Checking the time, I should still have twenty more minutes until she emerges from her in-home beauty salon.

Brandi remains quiet on the other end of the phone.

"Look, Brand-o," I continue, using the nickname I've known her by for as long as I can remember. Maybe it was a retaliation for her naming me Bratz. When those ridiculous dolls came out, the name was officially mine in Brandi's eyes. "I know you are looking out for me. I know all the reasons I cannot date Hads. But whether I do or don't is ultimately up to me. If I choose to get my heart broken by her, then that's that."

"You're smart, kid. You'll make the right decision for yourself," she says, nonetheless implying my smartness will lead me away from Hadley. I choose to let it go.

"Exactly."

"Oh, Michael wants to talk to you real quick. Something about a new house he's building."

She puts Michael Kelly, her husband, on the phone and we chat for a few more minutes about his design plans for a new house. He teases that I should join his company as his architect one last time before hanging up.

I rub the bridge of my nose, wishing I could join his company. But it's just not doable right now. Plus, I'd see my sister more often, and I'm not too fond of that right now after she has criticized Hadley so much.

My sister is the only one who doesn't root for Hadley and me to end up together. Brandi is friends with Hadley and knows all too well the type of woman Hadley is—a hot mess. Yes, I've dated around in my past, but Hadley....she leaves men shriveled up like a prune when she's done with them. No relationship of hers lasts longer than six months, well, besides *Daniel*. Even my internal thoughts sneer at his name. Hadley has issues, but I like to remind anyone who would dare bring up her past to me that we all have issues.

We all have some kind of past that we would like to forget.

CHAPTER FIVE

HADLEY

*B*reathe in, breathe out. You're okay, I speak to myself. Glacier eyes stare back at me. They know I'm not really okay. My hands remain plastered to the bathroom sink counter as I continue to calm myself down. Not only did Braxton catch me snoozing away in the t-shirt I stole from him while crashing at his place after a wild college night years ago, but he also saw my naked face. Rarely, if ever, have I let Braxton—or anyone—see me without a face covered in creams and powders. Only my two trusted girlfriends.

I suddenly feel eleven years old again, sitting in a lawn chair in front of my mama's small facial mirror. The memory is embedded in my soul.

"You're at the age now where you need to learn how to make your face pretty," Mama told me as she brushed through my blonde, wavy hair. She picked up a jar of creamy beige liquid, dabbed a brush in it, and stroked my face with the brush. "There, just your color. Watch how I do this so you can start doing it on your own. Don't

ever leave this house without your feminine power on full display." I didn't understand, but I watched her transform my face. It was like I aged five years because of the concoction of liquids and powders. I was obsessed.

In awe, I asked Mama what she did. "Hadley, baby. I made you into an irresistible woman. You're only eleven now, but one day, you'll need to be ready to attract a man that can give you everything your little heart desires and take care of you. This magical stuff will help you do just that."

I took those words to heart, not realizing the impact such toxic words would have on my developmental years. Rationally, I know that I'm fine and dandy without the cutest clothes, perfect make-up, and flawless hair. But Mama's words shot back to my memory as Braxton, with deer in the headlights eyes, took me in with my frizzy, tangled hair and bare face. And now, at twenty-seven, I still struggle to allow people—even someone as close to me as Braxton—to see me without my feminine power.

I guess it still wasn't enough though. Because right when I started to think I could genuinely be myself with a man who wasn't my best friend, he goes and picks a sleazy redhead to sleep with...just after he spent the evening celebrating six months with me. My heart aches, and I can't tell if it's more from the rejection, not feeling good enough, or because I actually miss Daniel.

"This is why I don't need a man to take care of me, Mama, " I say aloud to the woman looking back at me in the mirror. "I do well on my own. Better on my own."

But enough of that childhood trauma because I smell coffee...and eggs?

Transforming my face and straightening my platinum blonde hair, I shrug on my travel clothes—black leggings with a slouchy off-the-shoulder mauve sweater. Even though it's October, it's blasted hot in Mississippi. But I am determined to wear my fall wardrobe even if it's eighty-seven degrees outside. I will look good. I will NOT let myself go because of a stupid playboy man.

I'll be in my car for the most part, anyways. AC turned up all the way, my friends.

My phone rings with a call from Lorelei.

"Have you left yet? How's the trip?" she questions after I answer.

"Haven't left yet. Just finished getting ready." I laugh, but my inner thoughts berate me for not being ready when Braxton showed up. Why can't I just wake up and be on time for once? "You know me."

"I do know you, which means I know you slept in because you've had a rough time lately." Lorelei's words pierce me. How does she see right through me?

With a sigh, I say, "Yes, it's been rough. But I'm not going to let it get me down. I planned a fun road trip, and I'll have much more fun with Brax than I would have with Cheater Daniel."

"That's the spirit," Lorelei states. I vaguely hear the joy in her voice, but that's because I've trained myself to notice the slight inflections of her tone. She's a true female grump. No, not grumpy, I guess. Just...serious. All the time.

"Mom called. She's in prison again." I needed to tell someone. I didn't want to worry Braxton before this trip.

"Do you want me to check on her?"

"Please. I would appreciate that. I haven't answered her calls." My shoulders slump. I should have answered her, bailed her out. But then Braxton and Grandmama's advice from long ago comes back to me: If I truly love her, I have to help her see truth somehow.

"I understand," Lorelei says plainly. "I'll pop by the jail and make sure she's okay. Don't fret. She has to learn."

"I love you, Lor."

"Ditto," she says back in her regular voice, but I can hear the affection shining through.

Braxton

To my surprise, Hadley emerges from the bathroom with eight minutes to spare on the alarm I set for thirty minutes. That may be a world record for her, folks. But let me tell you, it was worth the wait. She is a beautiful woman without makeup, as I accidentally learned this morning. But now she looks like the woman I've been drooling over for the past twenty years. That one little porcelain shoulder peeking out from her sweater has my stomach in twisted pretzel knots. No wonder the modesty police tell women to keep their shoulders covered.

Who knew a shoulder could shoot tingles up my spine?

"Mmm, where's the coffee, Brax?" She sniffs, her petite, cute-as-a-button nose up in the air. *God help me,* I silently pray. I'm a goner.

"You need to ask a little nicer than that, Dawson." I hold her cup in front of me, giving it a good sniff. "Oh yeah, that's the stuff." Her eyes narrow, creating little crinkles in the corners.

"Give me the deliciousness." She holds a hand out while the other sits on her hip. Her all too curvy hip...

Snap out of it. You're riding a high from seeing her in your t-shirt.

"Ask politely." I wink, enjoying this new game with Hadley. Why did I wait so long to up the antics and actually *try* to make her mine?

"Please." The word hisses through pressed lips.

"Not nice enough," I say, bringing the cup to my mouth. I don't want to drink it. Hadley likes her sugar and cream with a dash of coffee, whereas I drink it black. But I guess I'll take one for the team. My lips fold around the rim as her eyes grow wide.

She sighs, dropping her arms by her side before muttering, "Please."

I take my lips off, thankful I didn't have to taste the Candy Land concoction.

"That's better." I smirk, handing her the coffee. Her eyes shift between the cup and me, and then she cements her stare on me while bringing the cup to her lips in the same place mine lingered moments ago.

Heat rushes up my neck and face as her full, pink mouth connects to the cup. I wish I was that cup of coffee.

She wins.

That is, until the coffee dribbles down her chin.

Laughter erupts from the pit of my stomach as she jumps backward holding the cup of hot liquid out in front of her like it's now a grenade that she can't let go of but desperately wants to. A curse slips through her lips.

I've got to say...she looks cute even with coffee dribbling down her chin.

"Language, Dawson," I snicker. She glares at me, setting the cup down and wiping her hands clean of the liquid.

She says that four-letter word a little louder. For the people in the back, I guess.

"You're trouble." I laugh, picking up my truck keys off the counter and dangling them in front of her. "Let's go."

Now, *she* starts laughing.

"You have a head full of stump water if you think we're taking your truck," Hadley says through exasperated laugher. She halts her laughs as if on command to take a careful sip of her coffee.

"There's no way you're driving us across the country," I state as she sets her cup down on the counter.

"Why? Because I'm a woman?" she questions, throwing her fists on her hips, one blonde eyebrow raising. *Really, Hadley?* I match her glare.

"Because you'll have us in the ditch before we even leave Mississippi." I turn my back and start walking towards the front door.

"Says the man who monster-trucked over a smart car two years ago." I stop, turn around, and walk back to her until we are chest to chest. More like her face to my chest the way I tower over her small frame. All I want to do is pick her up and wrap those short legs around my waist...

STOP IT. Back to mission: I Am Driving.

"Says the woman who has totaled three bicycles, two cars, and has killed countless innocent animals." She huffs out a breath accompanied with a dramatic eye roll, maneuvers around me, and grabs her keys from the counter. She doesn't hesitate to pull that corner of her lip up in a smirk as she dangles her keys in front of me, thrusting her hips behind her as she leans.

I love knowing what makes her tick. Peeved Hadley is just as attractive as, if not more than, Sweet Hadley. My body shudders just thinking about taking a few steps towards her, snatching those keys right out of her delicate hands, and showing her exactly what I think about "just friends".

Hadley grabs her bags like a pack mule and heads out the door, completely ignoring the eggs prepared for her. What a shame... Three perfectly good eggs gone to waste.

"Let's at least fight for it!" I holler after her, suggesting our game of Rock, Paper, Scissors.

The door slams shut.

This is going to be a *long* ten days.

CHAPTER SIX

HADLEY

Don't mind me. The silent tantrum I'm throwing—arms crossed, rose gold headphones smushed on my head, staring out of the passenger window and definitely NOT at Braxton's reflection—has everything to do with his perma-smug expression. Someone, please tell me how this man can hold a smug expression for fifty miles?!

So, how did I end up in the passenger seat of Braxton's truck?

I could blame it on Lorelei's text saying Mama was indeed locked in jail for drug usage. But honestly, that didn't shock me.

I simply suck at driving.

Though I would never admit that out loud to the gloating man.

I had won. Our luggage was tucked into my trunk. I held the victorious smug expression he currently wears proudly. I twinkled my baby blues at him in the passenger seat, threw my Jetta into reverse, and backed straight into the trashcan that I momentarily forgot was on the corner of the driveway.

Because it was stupid trash day.

He glared at me (I shrunk ten sizes), hopped out of the car to check for damage (there was none, thank goodness), put the trash back into the can (because he's a good man), and pointed for me to pull my car back into the driveway (yes, sir).

Why did I let my feisty feminine energy slip for a moment and listen to him?

Because you would do anything for Braxton Rawls, too, if you saw him vexed. With muscles bulging from his arms as a result of his clenched fists...that tense, sharp jawline...

I inwardly sigh, wishing I could make my best friend mine.

Why do I want him so bad now that I'm single? It's because he's hot. I'll leave it at that. Just my body having natural reactions to his good-looking self.

I dig in my purse for a lollipop, smiling to myself when I find my favorite flavor—strawberry shortcake.

But who am I kidding? It's not just because of his looks. Braxton is the man—the person, really—who has always been there for me. He's kind, hardworking, makes me laugh, and is gentle in the most masculine way. In the past when I have been single, I pined after him whether he was in a relationship or not (most of the time, he was). When another man came into my life, it halted the feelings for a while. But they never fully went away, so when said guy and I would break up, those feelings would come roaring back with a vengeance. And this breakup with Daniel seems to be no different.

No, I guess I didn't truly love him. Not in the way I love Braxton.

But no use in daydreaming. It can NEVER happen. Braxton can never be my rebound guy. Not to mention we are too different, and I am too used up. *Too much like your mama,* my inner voice whispers. I know he is waiting for marriage...and I surely haven't. And he is the man that deserves a woman who waited for him. Braxton is one of the good ones.

I catch his reflection in the window looking towards me, his smug expression finally falling away, replaced with...concern? A hint of worry?

This is another reason we would never work. Braxton seems to think it is his sole job in life to look after me. *Like a brother.*

Slipping off my headphones, Dolly Parton's voice fades away. The sound of some architectural podcast he's listening to fills the truck.

I peek through the waterfall of hair that I'd situated earlier on my left side to try and block him from my view, only to find him reflected in the window. *Sigh.* He's everywhere in this truck. Even his signature spicy, yet sweet, forest scent lingers in every fiber of fabric in this black truck.

There's no escaping him. It's enough to drive a woman to the brink of madness.

I watch him through my hair. His eyes keep drifting to linger on me, only glancing back at the road after seconds pass.

He pauses the podcast.

"What's on your mind, Bully?" Braxton asks. He reserves that nickname for when he is trying to be sweet or serious with me. I hated it for the longest time, but it grew on me. Endearing, of sorts. He calls me Dawson when he is perturbed with me. And then there's plain Hads like the rest of my friends call me. Oh, and Hadley.

I can't lie. I love the way he says my first name. Like an unspoken promise of things to come.

Taking the lollipop out of my mouth, I say the first words on my mind. "I gotta pee." My brain is looking out for me, even if it's a bit crass. *High-five, brain!* Because there is no way I can tell him what was really going through my mind. I'd rather talk about my urine needs.

He chuckles in a lively way, and his eyes pull back to the road for the sixth time. That's how many times he's flicked his dazzling green eyes at me through this conversation.

"Already?" We've only been driving for a little over an hour, but I already drank the coffee and an entire bottle of water.

"Yep. Gotta get my water intake in. Even on the road." I hold up the empty bottle with a shake.

"Thirsty much?" He wiggles his eyebrows, causing a lump the size of a chestnut in my throat. What has gotten into my best friend? He's never indicated before that he sees me as more than a little sister or a platonic friend. Dirty jokes are *my* thing. Flirting with him is *my* thing. Making him blush is *my* thing. This is not typical best friend banter.

Thank you, Cover Girl, for your ultimate coverage foundation, by the way.

It's working, right? No red splotches shining through on my cheeks?

I swallow the lump down, racking my brain for a remark.

"Only for you." I wink, satisfied when his face flushes redder than my signature Bad Blood lipstick. He swerves a little, then eventually takes the exit to the rest stop.

We are barely in Tennessee.

My entire body sighs in relief as I soak in the bubbling hot tub outside the Whimsical Romance cabin.

The six-hour drive to Pigeon Forge, Tennessee, took us eight hours. After my fourth water bottle, Braxton refused to stop for me anymore. He sheds his I'll-do-anything-for-you complex on long road trips, apparently.

His exact words to my inquiry about stopping to use the restroom were: "Hold it or I'll pull over and let you go on the side of the road. Your choice." My bladder is officially ruined for life. He could have caused me kidney infections or UTIs from that, and I was sure to let him know.

Mama called twice during the drive, and I didn't answer. Guilt began tugging at the edges of my consciousness after I denied her second call. Did I do the right thing?

Too late now, I remind myself. I take a shovel and bury the guilt six-foot deep, glad I still haven't told Braxton about her. He would have made me answer those calls and at least talk to Mama. He'd probably agree with Grandmama that I should leave her in jail, but he'd draw the line at ignoring her calls.

Trying to forget about Mama, I sink deeper into the hot tub. I booked this place for the trip—a one-room cabin for Cheater Daniel and me. The thought smacked me during one of our many stops, so I called the cabin owners while pacing a dirty gas station restroom floor. To my heart's delight and my brain's horror, they did not have a two-bedroom cabin available last minute.

I will be sharing a one-bedroom cabin with my best friend whom I want to desperately cuddle with and kiss and drown in comfort with. But I can't because he deserves so much more than my brokenness.

Not that we haven't fallen asleep together before on a couch when we were younger, but something has shifted between us. I can't pinpoint the moment it happened, but it happened. My best friend, slowly, over the years, has wormed a place in my heart and set up camp. And now I'm constantly throwing those pesky feelings out the window every time they come creeping back in. Especially now that I'm single.

Thankfully, the couch in the living room also serves as a pull-out cot.

We definitely could have been on the road longer today. He fought me when I told him we had made it to the cabin by three o'clock. In my defense, I booked it thinking I'd be spending the evening in a romantic cabin with my boyfriend, not my best friend. Who I want to cuddle all—

My phone buzzes on the edge of the hot tub, pulling me from the thought zipping inappropriately through my brain like an annoying gnat.

Braxton.

"Hey, are you in the bathroom? The light's on and I'm knocking, but no one's answering." His voice carries a tinge of concern.

He went for a walk when we got here to check out the pond. The man will end up fishing it before we leave in two days.

Two days.

"I'm in the hot tub right now. Must have left the light on." *Please don't, please don't, please...*

"Mind if I join you?" he questions, and I can hear the anticipation in his heightened voice. *Oh dear heavens.* Why am I so hormonal right now? Probably post-breakup energy.

"Come on," I say through clenched teeth. Dear universe, please let him come out fully clothed. Like top to bottom baggy, boxy clothes.

But heck, he'd probably make that look good.

"Great. Just let me change and I'll be right down." Click.

I set my phone down, take a deep breath, and fight the urge to slide under the water.

Waterproof mascara only goes so far.

I close my eyes.

"Hey." A man's voice causes my eyes to fly open and I sit up straighter in the hot tub. He's tall and well acquainted with the gym. His chestnut blonde hair is pulled into a man bun, but in a knotty, hasn't-seen-a-brush-in-months way.

Not attractive.

"Hi," I answer out of politeness. This is a public hot tub for the cabin residents, after all.

"I'm Johnston Rhodes." He pulls his white shirt off before sliding into the hot tub.

A little too close to me.

"Hadley," I say with a nod.

"No last name?" His brown eyes glint with mischief.

"Not tonight," I say before realizing how flirty it sounded. He scoots closer. "My boyfriend is on his way over here." I can't even bring myself to regret the lie that I so desperately wish was true because at that moment Johnston places a hand on my thigh.

He makes a show of looking around before saying, "I don't see him."

At that moment, I notice Braxton dash out of the cabin and head straight towards me.

Chapter seven

BRAXTON

Why am I going to join Hadley in the hot tub? One that I guarantee is crawling with germs and other disgusting content that I do not want to think about because cabins share it?

Because *Operation Make Hadley Dawson Weak in the Knees* is in full swing. It's still a working title, but you get my point.

I will endure the public cabin hot tub if it means getting to hear Hadley stumble over her words, get flustered, and not to mention her swimsuit.

Oh God, help me. I want to be a gentleman. But she makes it so hard.

I didn't even consider the swimsuit until this very moment.

Tugging the white t-shirt neckline, I chase away all thoughts of Hadley in a bikini. I think about Scripture, drilling operations, my dad...

Ah, that last one helped.

Shrugging on my swim shorts, I step out of the bathroom and begin walking down the stairs.

The cabin is cozy, warm, and inviting. It's similar to the one I'm building for myself—cypress wood, two stories, though mine is larger in square feet with three bedrooms. It has the same open-floor layout I have with the kitchen, dining, and living areas.

Hadley picked a great cabin to stay in.

The walk down the cabin stairs was too short. The walk to the outside door felt like a millisecond. And now I stand looking through the glass door of our cabin, surveying the area, trying to collect my wits. The hot tub sits in a courtyard shared with two other cabins.

With Hadley inside of it.

And another man sitting a little too close.

With emboldened fire, I throw the door open and make a bee-line for the hot tub. Hadley looks at me through her spider-like mascaraed eyelashes, innocent as apple pie. At my piercing gaze, the man slowly scoots away from her.

"Meet Johnston Rhodes from the cabin next to ours." Hadley's voice is thick and sweet as honey though her eyes convey discomfort. This guy looks like a weasel, and I'm not having it.

He may be a great person, but sitting with Hadley in the hot tub makes him Mortal Enemy number one. Am I going to have to punch another dude?

"Ah, the boyfriend," Johnston says, and I fight to keep my face straight and my eyes trained on the man instead of glancing at Hadley. If she called me her boyfriend, it must have been to get this man away from her. Though I can't lie, I love the sound of that statement.

"Yes, I'm the boyfriend. Braxton Rawls." I hold out my hand to shake his, which is perfect because I am standing opposite the two. He has to wade over to me to be a man and shake my hand.

Away from Hadley.

He grabs my hand, and I give it a none-too-gentle squeeze with a nod. Letting him know, clear as day, that this is *my* woman.

"It was nice to meet you, Hadley." Johnston squirms, his eyes still fixed on mine. "I better be on my way. Meeting coming up in an hour." He rakes over her with a sleazy look, gets out, and then nods to me saying my name once before grabbing a towel and walking away.

Braxton: one.

Johnston: zero.

"Boyfriend, huh?" I raise an eyebrow at Hadley, forcing the smirk down. She splashes water at me, and I chuckle before walking to her side of the hot tub. "We can make that happen."

Her face is flushed, but I'm not sure if it's from the heat of the water or my attempts at flirting.

"I didn't need your help. I could have handled him." She sulks.

"Sure you could have." I pat her head, continuing to laugh. She retaliates with a look that could have rivaled my mom's you-know-what-you-did-wrong stare. "That's why you called me your boyfriend."

She shrugs away from me, saying, "That's precisely how I was handling it myself. You just happened to be the man with me this time."

"Touché, Bully." I try not to think too hard about the fact that she said *this time* as if she goes hot tubbing with a bunch of other men on regular occasions.

Looking Hadley over myself, I see hot pink and porcelain skin through the bubbling water, and I notice she has a lollipop in her hands. Keeping a lollipop on hand is something new she's started in the past few months, and it KILLS me. I try to think of the way she would look with rotten, sugared teeth instead of the way her lips fold around the candy. My skin tingles like I'm in the middle of an acupuncture treatment.

I'm only a man. Time to get into the water.

In one practiced swoop, my t-shirt is off and on the floor beside the hot tub. The temperature outside sits around 68 degrees. Perfect autumn weather for a hot tub.

I slide in, sitting opposite Hadley, who has taken to staring at me.

"In the time that you called me, and I made it here, a man already zeroed in on you," I cluck, shaking my head. "Or was he here when I so rudely invited myself?"

"He wasn't here," she says hastily. "But you didn't have to scare him off with your grizzly size and death stare. He was getting too close and flirty, but I could have gotten him to leave myself."

So the man does suck. I shake my head again. "That quick, huh."

She shrugs, sliding neck-deep into the hot water, bringing her sucker back to her mouth.

Hadley knows she is a beautiful woman. A temptress.

But I also know she doesn't like the attention as much as she lets on. She likes to just be left alone.

Oh...

"Did you want to be down here alone?" I ask, realizing maybe she needed this time after being in the truck all morning and afternoon with me.

"It still feels like I'm alone when you're here," she says, and as much as I try to control it, my face falls. Ouch.

Her eyes grow wide as she slides up in the hot tub, that pink frilly bikini top surfacing.

I look away out of respect. But I still saw...

"I didn't mean it like that, Braxton. Oh my gosh!" She brings a hand over her mouth. After a beat, she says, "I meant that I'm so comfortable with you that I can be myself when you're around. I don't have to pretend."

"I get it." I breathe the words out, holding her gaze while sinking further into the water, careful not to let the water splash onto my face. "I can be just Braxton Lane Rawls with you."

"And I can be Hadley Anne Dawson."

We stay like that, her crystal blue eyes locked onto mine, until she looks away, a hint of a smile pulling at the corner of her naturally pink lips. She licks her lollipop, and I avert my eyes.

Her phone buzzes on the side of the hot tub, breaking the comfortable silence. She glares at the device before picking it up.

"You've got some nerve calling me," she growls to the person on the other end of the line.

I whisper the words, "Is that Daniel?" She curtly nods. I hold out my hand to take the phone from her, but she only shakes her head. After half a minute of listening to whatever he's saying, she turns her scowl toward me.

"I didn't tell him to do that, but it's not like you didn't deserve it," she bites out. Great. The sorry excuse of a man is ratting me out.

"Whatever, Daniel." She rolls her eyes. "You'll be fine. Man up." With that, she clicks off.

"Wanna tell me something?" she asks as she sets her phone back on the hot tub siding behind her. She crosses her arms, staring into my soul.

"Uh, I might have driven to Daniel's house before we left," I slowly say, testing the waters. They are murky and unclear. "And I might have punched him."

She throws up her hands, disturbing the water around her. "Why, why, why?" she groans. "I handled him. I did not need you stepping in. He's demanding you pay his medical bill, you know? His nose is broken!"

Despite the situation, I laugh. "I'm completely satisfied that I broke his nose. I'll happily pay for any medical bills. Dank Nose Daniel is his new name."

Hadley snorts a laugh, unable to hold it in. The water is clearing now.

"I can take care of my own messes," she says, but her cheeky grin lets me know all is forgiven. "But thank you," she finishes in a whisper.

"It was my fist's pleasure." The laughter dies down and we settle into another easy silence. The birds sing a song around us, crafting a tune that I commit to memory to copy on the guitar one day.

"This is kinda fun, huh? Getting away?" she asks, taking in the view around us. It is stellar. The mountains loom around us, the sun setting behind the western side.

"Kinda feels like old times when we would go camping in Dad's backyard. Mom would bring us marshmallows, chocolate, and graham crackers to our makeshift fire of sticks and dead pine needles." I reminisce. "Except no mountains like these. Only the sprawling woods."

"Don't forget her famous hot chocolate." Hadley and I both sigh with pure pleasure at the memory of the sweet, thick, chocolatey goodness. "Man, I really miss her."

My stomach lurches, and I feel like I might vomit right here. I press my lips together, keeping it in. "Yeah, I miss her too." The silence stretches on between us; the only sound is that of the bubbling water. Mom would have wanted this for me. She shipped Hadley and me before shipping people was a cool thing to do. Mom even gave me her ring before she died...

Why had I been running from Hadley for so long?

"Do you remember that time when we went to the Bluffs and stumbled upon the little pool of water?" Hadley asks.

Of course I remember that day. It was the first time I remember seriously thinking of Hadley as a potential girlfriend. She had cried her eyes out while we sat in the water because she had come home from school and her mom was strung out yet again. I had wrapped her in my arms and held her while the sun-heated water tinged our skin red. Her hair had smelled like coconut and her tears had dripped on my shoulders. Each tear broke my heart and

I remember thinking to myself, *"I want to be the person who always comforts her when she is crying."*

But what I finally reply is, "Yeah, that was an exhaustingly hot day. The hike to the pool was brutal."

"This weather is much better," she begins, adding the next part in a whisper, "and I'm much better."

"How is your mom?"

Hadley clenches her jaw then answers, "Fine as far as I know."

"You should call her while we're away. I'll be by your side just in case."

"Thanks, Brax. But I'd prefer to enjoy this trip."

Knowing better than to push her on this topic, I let it go.

I lean back, sinking further into the warm water, letting my muscles unwind and relax. It feels so right to be here with Hadley. Nothing replaces Mom, but being with Hadley dulls the ache. My head is light, my skin warm. Maybe I'm a little too comfortable?

Water assaults my face, and I jerk upright. I vehemently spit out the water (and germs) infiltrating my mouth. Wiping my eyes clear, Hadley's grin comes into full focus. I narrow my eyes, imagining they look like the slits in Voldemort's nose at this point.

"You did not just splash disgusting, germy water at me," I say the words slowly, honing my focus on Hadley. Our eyes lock. My prey will not escape.

I stand up, rising a full two to three feet above her seated position. My world spins a little, but I maintain my upright position.

Her grin slips.

"Rawls, don't you dare. I have my face painted on." Her words are rushed as she leans as far back away from me as she possibly can.

"Don't dish it if you can't take it." I cock my head and taunt her, inching closer across the hot tub to her. Why is the world spinning still?

"It'll smear!" she shouts, interrupting the evenings of the campers around us. Her lollipop falls to the ground outside the hot tub. "Look what you made me do!"

"You don't need makeup. Besides, what does it matter to ya? Got a hot date with Johnston tonight?" I step closer. Her breath hitches. Man, I love exploring what I'm capable of doing to this woman now that I've set my mind to making her mine. But what is she doing to me? I can't think straight.

I try to catch her hands, but pull back as she shoves more water in my direction. I take it like a man, trying *very* hard not to think of the microbes, and push forward. She stands up abruptly following the water assault, then she turns and scrambles to flee the tub.

Not on my watch, babe.

Whoa, where did that thought come from? Am I a "babe" dude now?

I wrap my hands around her waist, yanking her back into the hot tub. Except I didn't think this all the way through because the feel of my hands on her bare skin is short-circuiting my brain. My legs forget to hold strong, and she falls on top of me, shoving me into the germ-infested water—my mouth wide open.

Now I'm really going to vomit.

And I do, half in the hot tub, half over the side, in my attempt to get out.

CHAPTER EIGHT

HADLEY

I didn't plan to babysit a sick man on this road trip. Why do men act like the world is ending when they have a stomach bug? I've had plenty of viruses growing up. I even had to take care of my mama when she was too drunk to function, which often mirrored a stomach virus.

Taking care of Drunk Mom wasn't as bad as taking care of Sick Braxton. I pour a glass of Powerade in preparation for the next time he wakes up.

"Hadley," Braxton slurs from the couch as if my thought alone summoned him awake. "Can I have more Pepto yet?"

I check the time on my smartwatch, noting it's only been two hours since his last dose.

And it's almost midnight.

"Not quite yet. Two more hours," I say as I walk to the edge of the couch with a glass of blue Powerade—his favorite.

Braxton groans.

"Take a sip." I rub my fingers gently across his cheek, admiring his handsome face. One good thing coming out of this Sick Braxton experience is his new attitude. Gone is the man who controlled himself. In his place is a needy man who can't seem to be detached from me for more than a second. The neediness, though childlike and exhausting, makes me feel warm inside. I like that Braxton *needs* me. Black scruff prickles my fingers as I continue to graze his cheek.

"Open your eyes and take a sip," I repeat. "We gotta keep you hydrated."

He doesn't open his eyes. Instead, he nuzzles his cheek into the palm of my hand. Do I wish he would stay sick forever so that he would continue to need me? Yes, I do. And I'm unashamed.

But the man needs to hydrate.

I pull my hand away, and THEN his eyes open.

"Come back," he whimpers, turning his usually tan but now pale face towards me. I melt a little. Okay, a lot.

"Only if you start sipping on this Powerade." I never thought I'd have to withhold my presence from a man to get him to do something so small. I release a chuckle as I tilt the glass to Braxton's lips, his head meeting me halfway.

Even though he is sick, slightly smelly, and I've heard way too many sounds I never wanted to hear coming from him, I still can't get over how kissable his lips look.

I'm jealous of a dang glass.

"Okay, 'nough drink." Braxton sighs, grabbing my free hand that was just on his cheek earlier and pulling me on the couch to be his little spoon. "Come here." Thankfully, I had already set the glass down on the coffee table. He wraps his muscular arms around me, holding me quite tightly for a man weakened by sickness.

I wrinkle my nose at the scent of his sickly sweat and decide it's best to breathe out my mouth for a little while.

Because let's be honest, regardless of how he smells right now, I am very happy to be caged in his arms as he rubs his stubbly cheek against my head. Braxton feels like home. One that needs a good cleaning, but still home.

"Bully, you're my person," he mumbles, on the verge of sleep.

"You're my person, too, Brax." My heart beats wildly, though I know it's just the sickness talking on his end. *Don't let this go to your head, Hadley.*

I hear soft snores coming from the giant who's spooning me, and I determine I need a few more minutes to make sure he's fast asleep. Just in case.

Right after the vomit incident in the hot tub (which I am thankful to high heaven I don't have to clean up), I helped Braxton get back to our cabin. He beelined for the bathroom and hung out in there for a good thirty minutes before crashing on the couch. I got him settled, then took his truck out to buy a few things—Powerade, Pepto, crackers, and a thermometer—from a nearby grocery store. When I came back, he was in the bathroom again.

I took that opportunity to fluff out the pillows and throw a sheet onto the couch. He wobbled back into the living room with glazed eyes and only wearing boxers (sweet mercy, help me), and literally collapsed onto the couch.

I kept him up long enough to check his temperature to verify he did in fact have a fever, then I dosed him with Pepto I bought from the store and gave him ibuprofen from my purse. He's been in and out for the past four hours.

And every time he's awake, I'm summoned to his side.

Thankfully, the vomiting and dry-heaving stopped about an hour and a half ago. Hopefully, we are now in the safe zone.

His breath is even against my neck and the light snoring continues, so I wiggle my way out of his arms. I hope he is finished in the bathroom because I am in desperate need of a shower.

But the moment I slip out of his arms, I wish I could crawl back in. Where is this feeling coming from? Sure, my best friend is insanely attractive. He is the kindest, most gentle, caring man I know. But I've stopped my feelings in the past. Why can't I do that again?

Because you're tired of hiding it, my brain smugly answers.

It's just the maternal instinct from taking care of a sick person, I counter.

Liar, liar, pants on fire, my brain taunts.

Why in the world am I having this stupid conversation with myself?

Someone check me into a mental hospital, please, because I've gone crazy. Maybe a shower will clear my head. And my hormones.

I grab my pajamas, ready to get out of my bathing suit. I threw on baggy sweatpants and a t-shirt over my bikini to run to the store, and I never had time to change out of it between taking care of Braxton and contemplating if I should take him to a doctor. He vehemently opposed the doctor, so I've been playing nurse.

Ew, no. Not like that.

Not like I wouldn't mind though...

My mind, having zero control over itself this late at night, replays the image of Braxton pulling his shirt over his head like that scene with Ryan Reynolds in *The Proposal*. Apparently, my brain has a slow-motion feature because that's how I recorded the moment by the hot tub.

I fan myself again, something I've been doing on and off for the last few hours as Braxton flirted shamelessly with me in his needy state. I hop in the shower.

The shower does nothing but make me hotter. I quickly wash my hair and body in what has to be the quickest shower I've ever taken. I even turn the hot water down to a lukewarm level, but my body still refused to cool off.

The simple knowledge of Braxton sleeping twelve stairs down and seven paces out has my brain on high alert.

Yes, I counted when we first arrived at the cabin.

I needed to make sure I didn't stub my toe or trip if I had to run down the stairs to get him in case of an emergency.

Like an intruder.

Or spiders.

Like he'll be of any use in those instances now. I laugh to myself. Poor man. Stomach bugs suck. I hope he does as good of a job as I have taking care of him when the bug comes for me.

Checking the time, I wonder if Lorelei is still awake. I need some common sense in my life.

12:48 a.m.

Probably not. Maybe Lucy? I send her a text and am greeted immediately with a video chat response. Her wild, strawberry curls sit on top of her head in a bun, her green eyes bore into my soul.

"How's the Whimsical Romance cabin?" She wiggles her eyebrows. Stupid location tracking. Bad idea to call the romance queen.

"Okay, I'm turning off the location. Stalker." She throws her head back in unabashed laughter. I shush her to keep from waking Braxton up downstairs. *Gah.* He is so close to me...

"Go ahead. My plan is in action already."

"Lucy. What did you do?" She pulls a line across her lips with pinched fingers. "Lucy May Spence!" I holler in the most hushed tone I can manage.

"You'll find out tomorrow. Your text said you were staying in Pigeon Forge for two nights, correct?"

I narrow my eyes. "Yeah. But now I think I'll quit telling you things."

"It's nothing really. You'll enjoy the surprise being sent."

"You better hope so, Spence. 'Cause if not, I plan on getting sweet revenge one day." She holds her hands up in surrender.

"So," I continue, ready to sidetrack her. "How are you coping with Jake not proposing?"

She fiddles with a curl and laughs nervously. "Oh, it's nothing. Like y'all said. It's only been three months. Maybe month four." She finishes with another wink. The woman has a tendency to overuse the action. "But that isn't what you called me at nearly one in the morning to talk about, is it?"

Heat races up my naked face, and I know I'm glowing redder than Rudolph's nose right about now.

"Ooh," Lucy taunts. "Are my sweet friends already becoming lovers?"

"Not a chance, Luce Goose," I say, but my voice cracks a little.

"Come on, Hads. He is *perfect* for you."

"But I'm not perfect for him."

Lucy sits on the other side of the screen quietly. A rare feature for her.

"Nobody's perfect," she finally says. "But people do fit. Maybe I should say Braxton fits you. *Real* nicely." She drags the word 'real' out like molasses falling, a soft smile appearing.

And because I don't want to talk about this anymore (she was totally the wrong person to call), I burst out in a scream-whispered version of "Nobody's Perfect" by my beloved childhood superstar, Hannah Montana. Catching the memo, Lucy joins me and we have a mini Hannah concert before signing off.

But sleep still does not find me.

Because all I can think of is how unworthy I am of a good man like Braxton Rawls.

And questioning why I want him, anyway.

CHAPTER NINE

BRAXTON

Snap, crackle, pop. The classic cereal-named sounds make their way up and down my spine as I sit upright on the couch. I shake my hair out of my eyes, and the action sends a golf ball pinging around in my head. Why does my head hurt—

"Good morning, sleepyhead. How're you feeling?" Hadley's melodic voice drawls from behind me. I turn my head to meet her sweet smile and messy blonde bun, and everything comes rushing back in an embarrassing, terrifying flood.

I threw my guts (and probably my lungs and spleen) up last night.

And Hadley was there to witness it all...

There goes my chance at making her mine.

"I'm fine, just a headache. What time is it?" I ask, wiping the sleep away from my eyes. Is that rotten onion smell coming from *me?* Yep. There is no way Hadley wants me now...if she ever truly did at all.

"Ten-thirty," she responds, making her way over to me.

"Stop." The word flies out of my mouth before I can stop myself. Her brows knit together as she holds a coffee cup between her hands.

"What's wrong?"

"I smell." I sniff the air around me. "Like an onion. Seriously, my eyes are watering."

She laughs, throwing her head back in that cute little way she's done since we were kids. Then she walks to the couch anyway and takes a seat by me. Granted, she sits on the opposite end. Smart move, since my pores radiate the stench of what I assume to be the Grinch's after he chows down on onions.

"I took care of you all night long. I'm pretty much immune to the smell now."

"You did, didn't you?" The memories from last night play through my mind—Hadley placing a wet rag on my forehead, helping me take sips of blue Powerade and water, giving me medicine when I asked, and rubbing my back. I'm pretty sure we snuggled too, but maybe that was the fever playing tricks on my brain. "Did we...?"

"Hmm?" She takes a sip of her coffee, a hint of a smile playing at the corner of her lips.

"Did we...you know?" Her smile widens, showing off perfect, white teeth. Her mom didn't do much for Hadley growing up, but she did make sure Hadley got braces in middle school to correct teeth that were coming in twisted.

"Did we what, Brax?" She tilts her head, feigning innocence in her doe eyes. *You dirty player.*

"Did you have the best cuddling session of your life last night, even though it was with a surly, sick man?" Pink spreads across her cheeks, but she doesn't look away. She takes another sip of coffee, her eyes still staring into mine.

"Second best," she finally says. My heart sinks. Did Dank Nose Daniel still maintain first place position in her eyes? It's because I stink, not because I don't know how to be the best big spoon. Trust me, I can spoon. "Mr. Bear will always have first place."

Laughter erupts from me, and I revel in the mischief flashing in her eyes.

"I'll see what I can do to remove *Mr. Bear* from the throne." I wink, though the action hurts my head. Everything feels sore. Hadley's blue eyes crinkle in the corners as she laughs, but then a flash of curiosity appears.

"I look forward to it." She stands, leaving me to swallow the lump in my throat as she walks to the kitchen area in the small cabin. "I'm going to shower, then you need to take one before I go anywhere confined with you in that truck."

I watch Hadley walk to the bathroom, not missing the gentle sway of her hips. I'm pretty sure I said some things last night...things that I definitely shouldn't be saying to a person who is supposed to just be my friend. This road trip is going to be the death of me if I don't succeed in making that woman mine. Maybe it's time to play off my loose tongue brought on by my sickened state and up the antics?

I hear my phone buzzing on the wooden kitchen table. I stand up slowly, stretching my back out, then holler a thank you to Hadley for putting my phone on the charger for me last night.

I grab a cup and fill it with ice and water from the fridge before checking my phone.

A snap message from Michael.

Michael: How's it going?

Michael: Your sister made me ask dude.

Michael Kelly is the best brother-in-law I could ask for. He's been a solid male friendship in our small town outside of church members and the guys I work with. The rest of my time is spent with Dad, with Hadley, or with Hadley and the twins.

I imagine Brandi hovering over his shoulder, waiting for my response. Chuckling, I respond with a sleeping emoji.

Michael: *three coffee emojis*

I snap back with a picture of me sipping my water. I don't know if my stomach can tolerate coffee just yet. Though I do need to eat something. I find saltine crackers sitting by the couch on the coffee table.

Tears threaten my eyes as I think of everything Hadley did for me through that short, wretched sickness. She treated me just like Mom used to when I was little. Even when I was sick as an adult, Mom would come over and help me out. But it has been a while since I had someone look after me like Hadley did last night through my sickness.

The video call feature goes off with Michael's name but is undoubtedly my sister.

"Men." She snorts as our faces fill the screen. Michael laughs in the background.

"What's up, Brand-o?" I take another sip of my water before munching on saltine crackers. I hold my features intact. One wrong facial expression and Brandi will pounce like a mountain lion. I am cool. Antarctic ice chill.

"Curious as to how your little sub-in road trip as Hadley's boy toy is going." Direct as always. She likes Hadley, truly. She just doesn't think Hadley and I should be together.

She's the only one in this universe who thinks that, of course.

"It's good. We're staying in a cabin in Pigeon Forge. We'll be here for one more night. Probably going to explore the area today." Once again, Hadley has not let me in on the plans, no matter how many times I beg her. My streamlined brain feels all out of whack. I need order and plans, but I'm making an effort to go with the flow and make Hadley happy on this road trip she planned.

"A cabin? In the mountains?" Her eyebrows shoot up, hazel eyes searing into mine. I love that she has Mom's eyes. But every time she gives me this look, an ache rips through my chest. Where I look like Dad, Brandi is all Mom.

"Brandi. You know this was a trip she had—"

"Planned for her ex," she finishes. "I know, I know."

"So..."

"So be careful. Don't let the romance in the air sway you to do something you'll regret. You only stepped in to save her from going alone to this wedding."

"I know." I take a deep breath. "We are *just friends*. Nothing more. How many times do I need to repeat this?"

"Okay, okay. I'm just looking out for you. She'll break your heart."

"Just friends," I growl.

"Okay! Love you, Bratz."

"Love you too, sister."

Click.

"And what if I want her to break my heart?" I ask the cabin around me in a yelled whisper. "What if she wanted me here because I am *me?* Not because she would have been alone otherwise?"

Air. I need air.

I push open the kitchen window. "What if we are the ones meant for each other?" I half expect God to answer, but instead, the mountainous silence envelops me.

And then slow footsteps sound midway down the stairs.

I say a silent prayer that Hadley's presence is perfect timing and that she did not hear a word of that conversation with my sister or God's great nature.

CHAPTER TEN

HADLEY

The smell of fancy German beer penetrates my senses, churning my stomach and triggering my gag reflex. I clutch my lemonade between my hands and hold it close to my nose to curb the alcoholic scent. Why in the world did I plan this trip to OkTOBERfest? Oh yeah, Dank Nose Cheater Daniel liked beer tasting, even though I like to steer clear of alcohol due to my past. I take a sweet sip of my lemonade in an attempt to drown out the sour attitude.

Mama called again. I'm not sure why they keep letting her. I'll have to call the jail and ask Martin to tell her to stop and that I'll talk with her when I get back from the wedding. She always chooses to mess up her life when my life begins to make sense. It shouldn't make sense after catching my ex cheating, but last night happened, this morning happened, and now I'm delightfully confused.

Because unless I have been transported to an alternate universe where Braxton and I make sense, I've gone crazy.

I keep thinking I heard the words wrong. My best friend *surely* did not question, *"what if I want her to break my heart and what if we were the ones meant for each other?"* And by no means was *he* referring to *me*.

Except he was.

His conversation with Brandi, his sister, made that very clear.

Though I have to say I'm butt hurt over her comment that I would break his heart.

If I did, it would not be because I wanted to. I care about that man more than I care about my own life. If I broke his heart, it would be because I let him know he deserved better and needed to move on from me.

Braxton Rawls is better.

So much better than me.

But I have to admit, hearing those words come straight from his mouth shifted my mindset a little. Is it okay to entertain the idea of us? A version of us that steps right over the line of friendship? I think there's a possibility of an *us*...if I can get past my own *past*.

"You've got to try this Paulaner Weizen Radler brew." Braxton walks up to me from a tasting tent, pulling me out of my thoughts. He takes a sip and sighs, which makes my brain forget all the reasons I need to NOT flirt with my best friend who deserves better than me.

Turns out Braxton likes a good beer tasting too. Except he is only trying the non-alcoholic brews because he knows I don't drink.

"It tastes a little like oranges and lime." He takes another sip that ends in a deep groan of pleasure.

Oh my.

We would have adorable babies, just saying.

He holds out his sampler and I take a sip.

"Mhmm," I say, forcing the liquid down my throat. *Definitely* not my thing. Braxton releases his warm, carefree laugh. "Are you sure you should be drinking anything other than water and Powerade?"

"The bug was vicious but short. I feel fine now." He flashes a boyish grin that doesn't fit the scruff on his face and neck. "What are you drinking?"

"Classic lemonade." I beam and hold up my plastic cup.

"Living on the edge there, Hads." He laughs.

"Why don't you go taste actual beer? I know you like it. It's not everyday we get to come to a festival like this."

"Because I'm not going to put you into any kind of temptation to fall back into a lifestyle I know you want no part of. Besides, this stuff is way better than anything alcoholic." He casually shrugs, that boyish smile pulling at the corner of his lips again. My heart ruptures. I'm dead. Someone call the coroner.

Gah, stop! I can't take that smile on him, the one I've cataloged as the *real* Braxton. The happy, carefree Braxton.

"Stop what?" He smirks before continuing, "I am real, by the way."

Heck.

I went and spoke my thoughts aloud again.

I turn around, pretending I did not hear him at all. There is music, so that's a decent excuse. Though he must realize I'm avoiding responding because he snickers behind me.

"Let's go get a bratwurst!" I say a little too excitedly, turning away. Braxton bellows another laugh behind me.

"Y̲ou want another one?" Braxton asks as we both finish our second bratwurst.

"Maybe after I walk these two off." I pat my stomach. I need to find a bathroom and add a hair tie to the button on my jeans for a little extra breathing room. My head feels clearer after eating and my mood is definitely better than earlier. Despite my hesitations about coming here, I'm soaking in the fun and vibrant atmosphere.

Braxton, always the gentleman, takes my plate with his and tosses it into the trash can.

"I could have gotten that," I say. Though I love his gentlemanly behavior, I tend to feel the need to make sure he knows I am a fully capable, independent woman.

"I know, Hads." He sighs, running a hand through his thick, onyx hair. "Just let me do nice things for you anyways. That's all I ask." Well, okay then. My heart pitter-patters in my chest.

We walk around the festival, soaking in the atmosphere. Leaves crunch under my feet as a cool breeze tickles my neck. The foliage paints the mountains in the background a gorgeous mixture of reds, oranges, and browns. Scents of strudels, pretzels, and beer float through the air. German folk music tickles my ear, and all

I want to do is learn how to dance like the folk dancers wearing traditional dirndl (I'm learning a lot here).

"What was it like to live in Germany while all of this was the lifestyle?" I wonder aloud. Would I have been content and happy wearing one of those traditional dresses, living to serve my husband and raise children?

"I would have been a shepherd," Braxton says matter-of-factly. I stare at him incredulously.

"Why choose to be a shepherd?" I hold back my laughter at the image of this bear-like man herding sheep. Then again...it's kinda hot.

"I could be like David from the Bible. Insignificant in my status but with time to sit and reflect while out in the fields. The work wouldn't be easy, but I've never minded hard work." At that, Braxton looks down at me and grins. Does he consider being my friend hard work?

Way to jump to irrational conclusions, Hadley.

"You and that Bible." I snicker, shoving the previous thought down into a gopher hole. I grew up in the Bible Belt. Some would say that automatically makes me a Christian. I used to believe that, but now? How could a loving God leave me to the life He put me in? One of abuse and neglect.

A loveless life on all ends.

Mama still dragged me to church for Christmas and Easter services or when something else special was going on. Other than that, I haven't had much experience in a church.

Braxton, on the other hand, is the son of a pastor.

Just another reason we would never work.

"Have you heard the music David composed? His story?" he asks, knowing good and well I haven't.

"I guess I'll have to let you play for me at some point," I remark, hoping to change the conversation. His eyes light up when he talks about God, but it just makes me squirm and feel uncomfortable.

"I brought my guitar." He winks. *Oh boy.* I'm in for it tonight.

"Great." I roll my eyes. I do love listening to him sing and make music. He has a rich, masculine voice that caresses your body when he sings. But it won't be a love song he sings tonight. He will break out the Psalms.

I'll just have to distract him later.

"I would be a mom and a wife," I say, directing the subject back to the Bavarian lifestyle. "You know, because I'm a woman and that would be all that is offered to me."

"And that wouldn't be enough?" He stops mid-step to turn and face me. I swallow, his face inches from mine. When did he lean down like that? I'm swimming in a sea of green and the scent of woodsy pine mixed with beer and bratwurst.

"Maybe," I whisper. I'd be a much better mom than mine was to me. I hope I would be, at least. I'm not doing such a great job of not being her as it is. Snapping out of my trance, I add, "Or I could be a crazy cat lady."

He laughs, taking my hand like it is the most natural thing in the world. Does he even realize he's holding my hand?

"Crazy sheep lady. You hate cats."

"But why sheep?" I ask.

He stops us again, looks me square in the eyes, and whispers, "Because I'm the shepherd." Braxton squeezes my hand before leading us forward.

Well, he knows he's holding onto my hand.

But does he know that it feels like he is caressing my heart?

CHAPTER ELEVEN

HADLEY

B raxton and I stumble into the cabin in a fit of giggles.

I never took a sip of alcohol, so I know I'm not supposed to feel like I'm floating amongst the clouds right now. What. A. Day.

The only thing anchoring me to earth is Braxton's hand in mine.

I've held his hand so many times before. But today? Tonight? His hand feels like it was carved out just to fit with mine. Our fingers interlace perfectly, not an ounce of an awkward fit.

"Want to go to the hot tub again?" he asks.

"It's cooler tonight. Maybe we could stay in, get a fire going, and watch a movie or something?" I ask. He walks over to the stone fireplace and begins chucking the firewood that sat beside it into the furnace.

"What about giving you a personal concert?" he pipes up, holding a log out beside him like it's weightless while the other hand extends in the other direction. I would typically sit criss-cross apple sauce on the floor to listen to him sing and play. But I have a feeling it'll be worship music because of our conversation before, and I'm just not here for that tonight.

"Eh..." I say, mindlessly massaging one of my shoulders. "I'm tired and just want to chill. Rain check?"

"Sure thing, Bully," he says, tossing the last log into the fireplace. I try to respond, but I can't form the words. This could be our life if I let it. If I could get past my mistakes. My late teens and early twenties weren't pretty. I abused alcohol to numb the pain from *him*. From life. From the crappy hand I was dealt. I quit alcohol three years ago in my quest to be better than Mama. I healed eventually with the help of therapy, but I don't ever want to risk falling back into that dark abyss.

I watch Braxton start the fire. Better yet, I admire the way his arms bulge through his red flannel and the way his Wrangler jeans tighten around his bottom when he bends over.

Good gosh. Get a grip, Hadley.

Turning around towards the kitchen, I take a few slow, intentional breaths. Coffee. We need coffee.

I notice a basket of snacks sitting on the counter along with two bottles of apple cider.

Hmm, that wasn't there this morning.

The note has no name. Instead, it reads *"friends-to-lovers is my favorite trope"*.

Lucy. May. Spence.

I'm driving home right now to murder her. I'll be back before Braxton even notices his truck is missing.

"What's this?" I startle at Braxton's voice behind me. Plucking the note from the basket and stuffing it into my pocket, I practically growl Lucy's name.

"Huh, that's nice of her," he says, grabbing the cheese from the basket. "Shall I?"

"I'll get it. Go find a movie for us to watch."

I grab the sharp cheddar cheese and start working on crafting a charcuterie board. Yes, a board came in the basket. I find grapes, three other kinds of cheese, and several types of meats inside the basket.

The sweet, citrusy scent of the apple cider wafts upward as I pour two glasses. Might as well enjoy her little gift since it's here. Apple cider is one of my favorite autumn drinks.

It takes two trips to haul the food and drinks to the movie theater he has set up for us.

Braxton has the fire blazing hot in front of us, Netflix pulled up on the TV above it, a blanket and pillow pallet in front of the couch, and the two cushions from the sofa...indicating our seats.

He plops down on one of the cushions and then pats the other while gazing upwards at me.

Not looking at me like, "Hey best friend, come watch this movie".

He's *gazing*. Like Edward gazes after Bella. No, hungers.

His hooded eyes are a fire that makes my body hotter than the furnace in front of me.

Oh, heavens.

I take my seat beside him, careful not to touch him in any way.

After a few moments of scrolling through Netflix, we settle on *Sweet Home Alabama* and hit play. Braxton and I have been best friends for twenty years, so he is aware of my affinity for this movie.

What he doesn't know is why I love it so much.

Sure, the witty banter is on point. Reese Witherspoon is a goddess. Josh Lucas is drool-worthy. And a good enemies-to-lovers plot line keeps the romantic tension sky high.

But the real reason I love the movie? I always hoped it would be my story. With Braxton. Without the enemies part.

Childhood best friends who knew from a young age they would marry each other. Except if he would have asked me to marry him at eighteen, I would have accepted and been glad to have his baby.

As that infamous scene plays across the screen, I sneak a look at Braxton like a schoolgirl spying on her crush. With a side-eye glance, I catch him looking at me. Averting my gaze faster than the lightning striking the sand on the television, I silently hope he hasn't developed the power to read minds like Edward Cullen. On the other hand, I've always been an open book to him, and he reads me better than I read fashion magazines.

A giggle escapes my lips, and I decide to blame it on the sugar consumption from today and not on how elated my soul is. I blatantly stare at Braxton now while he watches the movie with a small smile tugging at his full lips.

"How many times have we watched this movie together?" I ask. He turns that smile towards me, and it grows wider than the double-wide I grew up in prior to Grandmama leaving me her house.

"Five, maybe six....thousand times." He laughs, a beautiful and deep carefree sound. It does warm things to my soul. I want to make him laugh more. It's my new life mission.

"Hmm, I thought for sure it was in the millions."

"Have you been watching it with another man?" Braxton asks, his eyebrows shooting up in a challenge.

"As if any man would willingly sit through a chick flick with me." I shove up against his arm, then decide to stay smushed up there.

"Chick flick?" Braxton brings his hands to his chest, his mouth agape. "I'm offended, Dawson. Are you telling me that I am a chick?"

"Brax. You are no more a chick than I am a thin supermodel."

"You could be a supermodel." Braxton playfully shoves the arm resting against him.

"Society *has* changed," I contemplate. "What face should I use?" I go through a string of faces, not leaving out the duck face, fish face, or chipmunk face. Why do we name so many faces after animals?

"Definitely the double chin." He tilts his head down, creating his own double chin, though I'm not sure how he managed that when he's solid as a rock. "That's my favorite." I nudge him again, letting my laughter flow freely.

Except I almost tumble over into his lap, catching myself with a hand on his thigh just above his kneecap.

All laughter ceases between us.

"If you want to sit in my lap," his voice develops a rasp as he leans his head down so that our noses are mere inches from touching, "all you have to do is ask." *Gulp.* My stomach twirls, the few cheese cubes and salami that are not fully digested are threatening to come back up. Not to mention the lemonade from earlier.

This better not be the sickness setting in. Not at this moment.

I am no more accustomed to Braxton's flirting than I am to experiencing four different seasons in Mississippi. It doesn't happen.

I can't let him keep getting to me like this. I've seen him flirt, of course. With more girls than I can count on my fingers. Sometimes it's like he doesn't even realize he's doing it. A pure natural at flirting.

I can do it, too. I'm just as good at it as he is. If not better. The best way to call his bluff? Accept the challenge.

"Braxton Lane Rawls." I tilt my head towards him, our lips only breaths apart. *Be still, my heart.* "May I sit in your lap?"

The darkness of the room clouds the color of his face, but I see I've got him by the way the apple in his neck bobs up and down. He pulls his face away from mine and tugs on the end of his flannel sleeve.

Bluff called.

With a victory smile, I begin to turn away from him and back to the movie. That is, until his hand reaches out and grabs my arm, stopping me from pulling away any further. With more force than I am used to, he reels me closer to him. He slips the arm closest to me around my waist and uses the other to form a cage of sorts.

Locked.

In the arms of my best friend who makes my head spin.

He picks me up with his brute bear-man strength and sets me down on his lap, not releasing his arms from around my waist. My body melts into his like butter on a biscuit.

We just fit.

"Your wish is my command," he whispers against my ear, using my own words against me. My body betrays me by shuddering from the tips of my toes up to the hair on my head. Like a wave of nerves shocking my system.

I have to put a stop to this. He deserves so much better.

But he feels so right.

CHAPTER TWELVE

BRAXTON

Flirting is a specialty of mine. I made no secret of my love of the game in the past. My teenage years were full of nonsensical flirting. As I came into adulthood, however, I dialed it back and only flirted with women I was interested in dating and pursuing. Women that could take my mind off wanting my best friend.

Meaning: I grew up and matured. That's when Jesus saved me, and my life really began to change. I recognized dating wasn't a game.

I have always kept my flirty side under wraps when it comes to Hadley. I tied up my flirting notions with Dyneema rope, the rope we use on the rig to lift heavy machinery, because if I started flirting with my best friend, I was sure to succumb fully to the love I felt for her.

She knows how to tease me right back.

We are not an opposites-attract situation when it comes to our interests. Hadley and I are two sides of the same coin. Outgoing, sometimes unintentionally flirty, and like to have a good time. We both love life and always want to make the best of it.

But where I grew up with loving parents, Hadley had a mom who loved the bottle more than her. She still doesn't know who her father is, and it forced her to grow up before she needed to. It hardened her heart to the world, but the woman still manages to be a vibrant ball of sunshine. Even through her dark spell at the beginning of college, she never failed to brighten my life just by being who she is.

Where I am a Christian, Hadley is skeptical about God. Rightfully so with her upbringing, but I wish she could see her worth through her Creator's eyes. To feel His love and know she always has someone in her corner.

But until she comes to that realization, I will be the man in her corner. I will love her. I will make sure she knows her worth.

And maybe through that, she will open her eyes to God. That's my prayer for her.

Did I ruin all of that last night? With my incessant flirting and ridiculous, irresponsible actions? I chose to challenge and banter with her because I *do* want to be hers. It isn't a game.

Tugging the neck of my sweater away from my skin, I let the cool mountainous air of Tennessee waft over me. We didn't *do* anything. Soon after I sat her in my lap because I'd lost my dang mind, we just sat there. No words, just listening to Jake and Melanie bicker back and forth on the screen. I enjoyed her presence, my arms wrapped around her waist. Her back relaxed against my chest like she belonged. It was as if she was Neil Armstrong and I was the moon. *Plant that flag, Hadley. You can stake your claim to me.*

We wrestled a lot as kids. That woman has never been one to shy away from a challenge, which meant that she'd end up tangled in my arms (to be honest, I ended up in hers because she continuously bested me before I discovered the holy grail of weights) and on my lap plenty of times. Last night, however, was not two kids wrestling and cutting up. It was two grown adults giving an inch into the emotions they were feeling. At least, I think her emotions were matching mine?

When the movie was over and my legs were tingling from sitting too long, I realized Hadley had fallen asleep. Her head had fallen into the nook between my shoulder and face, her breaths hitting my neck in soft, hot patterns. Drool dribbled down her chin, and I couldn't help but chuckle. Why was a sleeping, drooling woman in my lap the most beautiful thing I had ever seen?

I picked her up, limped around the room to gain feeling back in my legs and glutes while trying not to drop her, then carried her up the stairs. Tucking her in, I kissed her forehead and decided to admit the one thing I could never say aloud—*I love you Hadley Dawson. More-than-a-friend love you.*

Here I sit, back in my truck with the windows rolled down at Hadley's request, wondering what is going through that pretty mind of hers. Did she feel every nerve ending in her body light up like the Fourth of July as I did? Did she remember falling asleep with her back to my chest and her head nuzzled into my neck? Did she realize how I couldn't breathe throughout the entire movie because my body felt like it was going to explode like popcorn under prolonged pressure?

I glance over at her. She has rose gold headphones on and her feet propped on the dashboard. The sun pours through the window, lightening her platinum hair and reflecting off her tanned skin. She's bobbing her head along with whatever song is pleasing her—probably Dolly Parton—looking like a picture of perfection.

She catches me looking, and with a sly smile, she pulls her headphones down, strands of blonde hair caressing her face.

"See anything you like?" Oh yes. Yes, I do.

"Get your feet off the dash, Dawson." *No, keep them there. I like the view.*

"Let me drink water," she fires back. "And I would love more coffee. And for crying out loud...I need food."

I glance at the time. 12:48 pm. We have only been on the road for a little over two hours. Two hours left to get to her next planned stop—Charlotte, North Carolina.

"Yeah, we should probably stop for lunch soon. Need to keep Hangry Hadley at bay. Find somewhere on the GPS."

She sticks her tongue out at me like a three-year-old, but I can't complain. Her spunkiness and childishness are things I live for. Crave.

She starts typing away on her phone.

"But no fast food," I quickly add, knowing her affinity for McDonald's french fries and barbecue sauce. She looks my way, sporting a pout.

"I'll die if I don't get to dip crispy 19-ingredient golden fries into fake barbecue sauce." Hadley pretends to swoon. No way am I eating there.

"Fight me for it?" I suggest, glancing at her in time to see her eyebrows shoot up. She can't resist it. She sets her left hand out in front of her, palm open, and places the right on top of it in the rock position. Since I'm driving, I take my right hand off the wheel and put it into the rock position over the air between us.

"Rock, paper, scissors, shoot," we say in unison, a practiced dance.

She pulls rock, as is typical for her first round. I pull scissors, always satisfied to give her the first win. *Point, Hadley.*

"Rock, paper, scissors, shoot."

I draw a rock as she draws scissors. Point, Braxton.

Now for the kill. She'll pull paper, and I'll pull scissors.

"Rock, paper, scissors, shoot."

I lay my hand palm down over the air, and she...pulled rock again?

"You cheated," I accuse. We do this jig all the time and rarely does she change things on me.

"Really, Rawls?" she bites out. Hangry Hadley is coming out to play. "I know your game. Do you think you have me figured out? Well, you're wrong. And I choose McDonald's." The rumble of the road beneath my tires is loud.

"Fine. But at least find me a Subway or something."

"Or something," she mumbles under her breath, typing away on her phone again. I reach for the radio and turn up the music. A new country song plays through the truck speakers with lyrics about a man being a boyfriend without benefits. I risk a glance at Hadley, who's still buried deep in her phone, and slowly turn the music back down. No more of that while she's here, but I make a mental note to google the lyrics and artist later. Does she even realize that's what I am to her?

We continue the drive in silence.

Before I know it, we are both sitting in an old-school McDonald's booth. Hadley is munching on a burger and fries—she actually sighs while eating—while I sip on sweet tea and take small bites of my chicken bacon ranch salad. I'm not a health nut by any means, but I do watch what I eat. Watching my grandma suffer from type two diabetes, the shots and insulin and attacks, was imprinted into my mind. I did not want to have the complications she did if I could prevent it.

There was no other option than Mcdonald's. At least, that's what Hadley said.

"Want a fry?" She holds a long fry and wags it in my face. She's chipper now that food has entered her system. "Seriously, Brax. Treat yourself every now and then."

"With thin fries from McDonald's?"

"Precisely," she says, dipping it into her barbecue sauce and shoving the fry into her mouth with a cheeky smile. I love this smile—the one where her eyes crinkle up, her cheeks rise, and her chin tosses up slightly. Who am I to deny the apparent bliss a french fry can give her?

"So, what's on the agenda for Charlotte?" I ask. She dabs at the drop of barbecue sauce that fell from a fry onto her blue sweater. The same deep blue color of her eyes.

"A new Chantilly sweater." She sighs. "Seriously. Why can't I eat food or drink anything without getting it all over me like a baby with her first birthday cake?"

"Because you're Hadley." I shrug. This is nothing new. Nor as bad as the time she tripped and reached out to the counter to prevent her fall. But instead of grabbing the counter, she grabbed the low-carb pie she had made me for my birthday. There were many tears from her and concealed laughs from me that night three years ago.

"I'd like to trade me in for an updated version."

"I like this version." I wink. She rolls her eyes, but I don't miss the way she turns her face away as a smile forms across her signature pale pink lips.

"Amusement." She laughs, her smile morphing into a smirk. "That's what's in Charlotte. You'll hate it."

CHAPTER THIRTEEN

HADLEY

*H*e *"more-than-a-friend loves me."*

At least my dreams tell me that. But it was oh so real. I could still feel the way his breath tickled my ear as he whispered the words. I felt it down my spine to the tips of my toes. Everyone's favorite mall song—"Bubbly" by Colbie Caillat—has played on repeat since that unfortunate dream.

Speaking of tingly feelings...

"My body's in overdrive!" I yell over the roar of the rollercoaster as it drops down, taking my stomach with it. Braxton's face is literally turning green, and I'm seriously afraid he may barf all over us. I don't need a repeat of the hot tub, thank you very much.

After we checked into our hotel in Charlotte, North Carolina, I forced him to let me drive to our evening destination—Fableland Amusement Park. Daniel loved amusement parks. Quite frankly, so do I. I had planned this time for us to have some fun...before he decided to have fun with another woman.

Shake it off, girl. You're Taylor Swift. He isn't worth your thoughts.

But Braxton? He hates amusement parks. Grinch-style LOATHES them. I promised him his restaurant of choice if he would ride one roller coaster with me. After we watched one group stumble off the nearest coaster and another group eagerly get on, he reluctantly marched over to stand in line for that coaster—Flashtime, one of the fastest, tallest rollercoasters. The one I had conveniently situated us near before making the deal.

I never said I played nice.

When the coaster comes to a halt, one look at Braxton has me bursting at the seams with laughter. His usual gel-styled, slicked-back hair sticks up in wild directions, matching the panic swimming in his dark roast eyes. His hands are glued to the safety rail, which is rising as the operator brings it up. I reach for his hands, prying them from the continually lifting metal bar.

The man looks absolutely shell-shocked. Coaster-shocked?

He shakes his head suddenly, coming back to reality. He stares down at our jumbled hands, which currently look like a Hadley Hand Sandwich the way his are squished between my own.

Feeling the heat rush to my cheeks—or maybe windburn—I snatch my hands back and hop out of the cart.

What a rush.

The rollercoaster, not the intense hand-holding.

Okay, maybe both.

"I'm gonna be sick," he says, swaying as he takes a few steps away from the ride to lean against the fence. "Again."

"Good thing I brought Dramamine," I hold the tube of pills up and give it a shake. Poor thing. I guess I should have taken into account he had a stomach bug only two days ago before forcing him onto the coaster.

"Why in the world did you not give me that *before* the ride?" He questions me like he's trying to be mad, but is too sick to muster up the correct level of irritation.

"Couldn't have you guessing what we were up to." I grin. "Or else you would have never agreed."

"Dang right I wouldn't've agreed." He snatches the tube from me and manages to get a pill out. He takes it without a drink. Such a man.

A hot, motion-sick man.

"Do I look that bad?" he asks, a slight scowl painting his face.

"Hmm?"

"You were staring."

Oh.

"I've never seen your hair so out of place." I titter, massaging my shoulder while averting my gaze. I definitely was *not* thinking of what it would be like to push him against the fence and kiss him until we were both dizzy again.

"Mine? You should see yours." He chuckles, taking a hand and tucking the flyaway in front of my head behind my ear. "But actually, I kinda like this version of you. Free. Not completely dolled-up." Okay. I am *totally* thinking about shoving my best friend against the fence and devouring his face.

I must have done a heck of a job with my *woke-up-like-this* makeup this morning.

I take a step back away from his hand that lingers at my ear, his fingertips tickling my skin.

Distance. I need distance.

"Want to try out Dorothy's Cyclone with me?" I laugh off his compliment. Compliments and I have never been friends. Often I will fake a thank you with a smile, but deep down, my brain screams that the compliment is not true.

"Yeah, no. Not gonna happen, Dawson. But I'll happily sit and watch while I eat a soft pretzel."

"A pretzel?" I feign shock. "You're living on the wild side today, Rawls."

"To settle my stomach," he adds. "I'll take a sprite, too."

"Imposter!" I point with a gasp. "What have you done with my health nut best friend?"

With a sigh, he says, "I'm right here." Is that a frown?

I elbow him in the side. "Buzz kill, man. What's up?"

With a forced smile, he shakes his head to say nothing and starts walking toward the pretzel stand.

What was that about?

My phone buzzes in my pocket. Taking it out, I see Lor-A-Lie flash across the screen for a face chat call.

"Hey, hey, Lors!" I answer the phone with a grin. "Guess what? Brax is fixing to eat a carb-loaded pretzel...AND drink a Sprite!" I snicker while Braxton glares in my direction.

"Hey, Braxton!" Lorelei shouts from the other end of the line. I flip the screen so he can wave at her from in front of me.

"What's up?" I ask.

"Nothing much. Just wanted to touch base with you about Rose Lynn." Braxton slows his pace, and I equally slow mine.

"Can we talk about it later?" I plead silently with Lorelei to understand. I don't want to tell Braxton that Mama is in jail again. Or that I haven't talked to her.

Lorelei narrows her eyes, then says, "Sure."

"I made Braxton ride a roller coaster," I quickly change the subject. She snickers, and I flip the screen back to Braxton who has now stopped in his tracks and is looking back at me. He wants to ask about Mama, I can tell, so I'll just have to preoccupy him some other way.

"Did you have fun?" Lorelei asks Braxton, whom I've caught up with.

"I'm fixing to shove a pretzel into my mouth and down it with Sprite. What do you think?" he snaps, but a playful smile tugs at his lips.

"Point taken," Lorelei says. "Well, you two kids have fun. I hear Lucy screaming in the background. Better go tend to her."

"What's wrong?" I ask. Braxton and I get in line for pretzels.

"Jake broke up with her like five minutes ago. She hasn't calmed down enough to earn her phone back, so that's why she hasn't texted you yet." Lorelei waves Lucy's phone in her hand.

"Should I talk to her real quick?"

"Better not. Not if you don't want the entire amusement park thinking you have psycho friends in your life."

"Text me when you give her the phone back so I can call," I state. My heart sinks like a rock thrown into water. Lucy seriously liked

Jake. She thought he would propose. This isn't going to be fun to walk through with her, but I will because she is my best friend.

"Will do." Lorelei clicks off. Before I tuck my phone away, I see a text come through from her saying Mama is okay.

Not good. Not doing well. Just...okay.

I shake the feeling that I need to call Mama away in favor of ordering a pretzel.

After munching down a heavenly salted pretzel smothered in hot cheese (Braxton refused the cheese, which meant I had double), I make my way to stand in line for Dorothy's Cyclone.

The autumn breeze carries the smell of hamburgers and popcorn, making me hungrier than ever despite the pretzel I had just ate. I check my phone, shoot a few work emails off, and text Lucy back (she wrestled her phone away from her twin) letting her know I'll be free to talk later. A hand taps me on the shoulder, causing me to whip around faster than the tilt-a-whirl here.

"Hadley Dawson?" the man asks. His eyes—a rich, sapphire blue—are a color I have only seen on one other human being in my life.

"Oh my gosh!" My mouth drops to the floor. "Finley Andersson?"

"Yours truly." He bows like the prince he is. And I mean it. He is a prince. Second in line to the throne of a small European country with Swedish roots called Korsa. Only a handful of people from college know about him.

"What are you doing in North Carolina?" I look around, realizing I am standing in line for a roller coaster. "At an amusement park?"

"What? Princes cannot enjoy the amusement of carts on wheels going forty-five miles per hour?" His blonde waves ruffle in the wind. His accent has Americanized more than the fake one he sported in college.

"Who are you here with?" I wiggle my eyebrows. The man had every woman falling over their sneakers in college. We never dated because there was zero chemistry between us. But the friendship came as natural as pouring hot syrup on pancakes.

Dang, I need to get more food. That pretzel didn't cut it.

"My baby sister, Astrid." He motions over to a young girl—probably late teens, maybe twenty. She looks exactly what I imagine Finley to look like if he was a young female. "She came to visit me here and wanted to try a rollercoaster. I live in Charlotte now."

"Why?" I mean it as an honest question, but it comes out in disgust. Because how can a stinkin' prince—a man of ROYAL blood—want to live in Charlotte? Or anywhere that is not a palace in general?

"Come on, Hads. You know me." He places a hand on my shoulder. And I do know him. He hates everything about being royal and in the spotlight. He has stayed out of it most of his life, earning a reputation in Korsa as the reclusive prince of hearts.

Rumor has it that he's been off jet-setting the world, stealing hearts and crushing them beneath his handsome, charming teeth.

Yeah, no.

As far as I know, Finley hasn't dated a single woman while he's been in America. Then again, I haven't seen the man in over four years since the last time we ran into each other at a coffee shop in New Orleans.

A throat clears behind us as Finley takes his hand off my shoulder.

"Do you know this man?" Braxton steps between Finley and me, his voice a low and deep warning, as he glances back at me before boring his eyes into Finley. At least, I assume that is what he's doing as the giant of a man is blocking my view of Finley.

I step to the side of Braxton to give proper introductions. "Braxton Rawls, meet Finley Andersson."

Finley reaches to shake his hand while Braxton stares at it like it's a bomb that'll explode with the briefest of touches. Finally, he reaches across and gives Finley's hand a firm shake.

"Sorry, Fins. Braxton doesn't mean to be a brute. He thinks you're some rando guy trying to seduce me," I state. He still doesn't divert his gaze from Finley.

"So," Braxton begins, caution still plaguing his tone. "How do you two know each other?"

"We met in college at Ole Miss," I begin when Finley cuts in.

"I saw Hadley trip while walking across the courtyard. Her books went everywhere, along with the cup of coffee in her hand. People either ignored her or snickered, so I ran in to be her saving *prince*." Finley teases the word with a wink at me.

"Did you two ever date?" Braxton outright asks him, then faces me. "I don't remember you mentioning him before."

"Like it's your business," I snap. "But no—" I say right as Finley shouts "no" a little harshly for my liking. "What would be wrong with dating me?" Good luck with that answer, pal.

"For one, there was this guy named Braxton Rawls that you never quit rambling on about." Finley flashes a smile at Braxton. "I am happy to see you finally won him over."

SOMEONE SHUT THE PRINCE UP.

"I—" I begin, but what are words? Finley Andersson, Prince of Korsa, just ratted out my dearest secret to the one person my secret had no right going to. As my face grows hotter than black asphalt in the dead of a Mississippi summer, Braxton smirks. I only see it out of the corner of my eye because I am currently refusing to look his way.

"Finley." Braxton practically sings his name. "You are my new favorite person." Finley tilts his head as if trying to figure out Braxton's sudden change of mood.

"Next!" The ride conductor calls, and I slide into the cart with Finley getting in beside me.

"I thought you were riding with your sister?"

"She went on one and refuses to go on another," he states.

"Well then. That gives me plenty of time to yell a string of southern curses to your pretty little face." I throw a smirk in his direction as the metal bar lowers to secure us in. "No way out now, Fins."

CHAPTER FOURTEEN

BRAXTON

*T*hank You, God, *that I am not in Finley Andersson's place at this moment.* I stand amused against a fence as I watch Hadley scold him, alternating with a wagging finger in his face and her arms flying with her words as the roller coaster goes round and round. No doubt the miserable soul is getting a mouthful.

Me?

I'm throwing a parade in my head. Trumpets are blasting, confetti is flying, and drums are beating.

Hadley Dawson never quit talking about me in college.

Those years filled me with dread as I watched her come home time after time with a new man, certain one would put a ring on her finger at any given moment. I had just surrendered my life to Jesus, and I had to focus on my walk with Him, no matter how much it hurt to watch Hadley with alternating men on her arm.

Hadley Dawson never quit talking about me in college.

I have to remind myself that college was six years ago for her. Feelings can change in six years. Mine did. They grew astronomically. My love for the woman runs deeper than the oil deposits I manage.

But anything she felt for me could have disappeared. I could have waited too long. Then again, I'm the one on the road trip with her. She could have called up an ex, or taken Lucy or Lorelei. But no. She asked me. Braxton Rawls. Her guy best friend. The one who is trying to be *so much more.*

The buzzing in my pocket pulls my attention away from Hadley's angry show.

"Hey, Dad."

"Hey, son. What's that noise? How's the trip going?" His voice is tired and worry immediately consumes me. He's been spreading himself too thin and refusing to ask for help.

"Going good. We are at an amusement park in North Carolina," I say.

"You? An amusement park? She's got you wrapped, son." My heart beats triple speed because he's not wrong. And I need to fully admit that to myself if I have a chance of winning her over. I do not have to admit that to Dad, however.

"What are you up to?" I say, derailing his current line of thought.

"Oh, not much." I hear something in his voice that sets me on edge. He is tired, but there's something else. "I chatted with Patton Harrison at lunch, and he said—"

"Dad. I've told you I wasn't interested in a career change." Deception. That's what laced his voice.

"I know, son, but—"

"No, Dad. With all respect, no."

"Okay, okay. I hear you." No, he doesn't.

"Braxton!" Hadley calls, stumbling off the roller coaster. Finley looks whiter than a ghost, but it's his expression that looks as if he just sat through *The Conjuring* that throws me over the edge. My heart goes out to him. I remember this one time during my senior year when Hadley, a feisty sophomore at the time, got upset with me for pranking my English Literature teacher. I, with the other seniors (because it was senior prank week), Saran wrapped everything in her classroom. Hadley was close with Mrs. Poolson and gave me (and the other guys) an earful for doing that to "the sweet old lady". That lecture was one of the more intense Hadley Lectures I've been on the receiving end of. It looked very similar to what Finley was getting on that coaster.

"I gotta go, Dad. I'll check in tomorrow morning." With a huff, he grumbles that he loves me and hangs up.

"Who're you talking to?" Hadley bounces to my side, acting like my entire world didn't just shift when Finley let her little secret spill.

"Just Dad," I say, cooler than a lick of ice cream on a summer day. She doesn't want to talk about it? Fine. For now.

A female version of Finley glides up beside us, and he introduces the young girl as Astrid Andersson, his sister.

"It is nice to finally meet you, Hadley. Finley has told me so many stories involving the two of you in college." Astrid's smile is soft as she embraces Hadley. "And who are you?" She eyes me up and down. I squirm a little because she has to be like, maybe twenty? Way too young to be perusing me like that.

I hold out a hand. "Braxton Rawls."

"It is nice to meet you," she says with a grin before turning back to Finley. "Let's go to the souvenir shop."

"It was nice to meet you, Braxton." Finley holds his hand out, looking like a scared puppy in a thunderstorm. I grab his hand with a firm shake, letting my eyes convey my gratitude. A smile tilts at the edge of his lips, and I know we have an understanding.

"You too, Finley."

"Well, Braxton, we better get going." Hadley starts maneuvering through the crowd.

"You've only ridden two rides." I fold my arms across my chest, offering a challenge as she walks away. Want to talk about it, Hadley?

"Yeah, but I'm not eighteen anymore. Can't handle it like I used to," she says, digging through her little backpack. She pulls out a lollipop, unwraps it, and brings it to her lips. Then she turns around, heading towards the exit with a quick march.

As I watch her walk away, testosterone takes over. Nope, she is not eighteen anymore.

And twenty-seven looks dang good on her.

We didn't make it five minutes in the truck on the road towards the hotel before Hadley spotted a coffee shop with a mural on the outside that read "drink the bean, achieve the dream" and had to stop for a picture. After twenty minutes of me finagling her phone trying to capture that "just right" picture, I decided we could both use a cup and the owner could use our money for the chaos that ensued outside the coffee shop door.

"Heaven in a cup," Hadley coos to her drink before taking another sip of the caramel vanilla latte with almond milk. "This was a *great* idea, Braxton."

"That's me. Full of great ideas," I take a sip of my black drip coffee. There is an awkwardness between us that didn't exist prior to Finley's secret-spilling moment. I decide it's time to address it. "So...Finley Andersson, Prince of Korsa..." She simply stares at me, so I add, "How does a prince find his way to Mississippi?" She had told me about his secret as we left the park.

"When he first opened up to me about his *status*, I asked the same thing." She chuckles at some memory playing in her head. "Turns out, he met some Mississippi folks back in Korsa and wanted to experience their lifestyle. So of all the places he could have gone to college on exchange, he chose the University of Mississippi."

"While I find plenty of fault in his school choice," I begin, taking a shot at her alma mater. She sticks her tongue out at me, and I resume, "Our state is a great one. It has its own culture of sorts."

"That's what he said," she reflects. "Of course, he met me right off the bat, so he got *real* acquainted with our way of life." Hadley plays with her coffee mug like something is bothering her, and I know she is begging and pleading that I won't ask the question that's coming next.

Too bad, Hads.

"About what he said…" I begin, and her finger freezes on the rim of the mug. I mentally will her eyes to look at me, and it works. I stare into her baby blue crystals. "Is that true?"

She clears her throat, her pink lips parting. *Eyes off her lips, Braxton.*

"You're my best friend." She shrugs. "Of course, I never shut up about you." My heart sinks. She has a point. Maybe it wasn't what I made it out to be.

"But why did he assume we were dating?"

Again, she shrugs. Her eyes shift back to the mug in her hand as she responds. "Beats me. I guess because we're here together. Just us."

"Yeah, guess so." I huff, shoulders falling. Surely I wasn't making all her nervousness up in my head. I know Hadley loves to flirt with me, but it's because it gets under my skin. Or it used to before I decided to flirt back. There is chemistry here, though. She has to feel it. I'm not giving up just yet, but I do let it go for now.

For now.

"You know what this day reminds me of? The last time we went to a fair together?" Hadley asks as she swaddles the coffee mug between her hands.

I smile, hoping it's the memory I'm thinking of. "The Juniper Grove county fair?"

"Sixth grade." She takes a long sip of coffee, shifting her eyes away. I mimic her actions except I keep my eyes glued on her, watching her subtle movements.

"Do we talk about that day now?"

She shrugs. "Why not? We're mature adults."

"The day Hadley Dawson became a woman. In front of the entire town."

She rolls her eyes with a laugh, then meets my eyes, all traces of humor gone. "You were so good to me that day. While everyone else shouted quite creative names for the girl with crimson on her white pants, you took care of me. You didn't care about your reputation or ego. You were just...there."

"Where else was I supposed to be?" I knit my eyebrows together. "You needed me."

"Despite the unusually cold night, you wrapped your jacket around my waist. Then you bought me a pretzel and walked me home." Hadley sighs, rubbing her forearm. "You've always been there. Here. And I don't think I've said thank you. So...thank you."

Dumbfounded, I search for a response while I search her tear-filled eyes, trying to find the more-than-a-friend love there. Nothing other than *"I love you, that's why"* feels worthy enough to be said right now. I swallow the lump rising in my throat. This is my opening. The moment I could confess everything and get on with my plan to make this woman my partner in life.

But the second my lips part, the door to the coffee house swings open, bells chiming.

Moment over. Hadley shakes her head as if waking up from a daydream. Because maybe that's all we are... an unattainable dream.

No, that's not right. There is so much more to us, but it can wait just a little bit longer.

"Ready to get back to the hotel for the night?" I ask.

"I got about a quarter of a cup of coffee left, Rawls. Don't rush my coffee drinking," she threatens with a smile, back to her pre-memory lane self.

"Down, Bully." I hold my hands up and lean back, as if releasing the desire to spill my guts here and now in the simple motion. She grimaces before throwing the rest of her coffee back.

"Alright, Rawls." Hadley stands and begins walking out of the coffee shop. I watch her walk away for the second time today. She flings her head around to smirk at me. "You coming? Or are you just going to keep watching me walk?"

Heat flashes up my neck, and I stand up and follow after her, nodding good day to the barista who is holding back a laugh. I hear the laugh let loose as the coffee shop doors swing closed behind me. The icing on the cake? That song about being a girl's boyfriend without the benefits is playing on the patio speakers outside the coffee shop. I researched the singer and lyrics while Hadley finished her McDonald's food earlier, and I've adopted the song as my anthem. *Thank you, Mason Kane.*

Chapter Fifteen

Hadley

Braxton is in the shower right on the other side of this very thin wall. I can hear the water droplets hitting the floor of the tub and...

Oh dear heavens. Someone shut my brain off!

I fan my sweltering face with both hands while relocating myself to the other end of the small hotel room. One that only has one bed because again, this trip was planned for a romantic couple. Not a girl and her best friend who could be featured on the Hunks of Hallmark Instagram page.

My phone buzzes in my back pocket, so I take it out to find Lorelei calling me to video chat. I answer, and Lucy's wide smile and Lorelei's soft smile greet me.

"Sorry we didn't text back earlier," Lorelei says.

"Did you two kiss?" Lucy questions me right as Lorelei finishes speaking. She bumps Lorelei out of the screen and grabs the phone. "What? Look at her flushed face!"

"Lucy!" Lorelei barks before wrestling the phone back from her twin. Lucy shouts something about needing this conversation to distract her from Jake.

"Uh, ladies?" I interrupt their bickering, obliging Lucy's request. "We have a problem."

"You're in love with him, aren't you?" Lorelei asks, shocking me. My heart speeds up hearing someone else say those words.

"Duh." Lucy rolls her eyes. "We *aaalll* already knew that. Besides them, of course."

"Pipe down," I hiss. "He's in the shower and these walls are paper thin."

Lucy wiggles her brows and makes kissy faces while Lorelei smirks with a nod of approval.

"Fine, yes. I'm in love with my best friend," I whisper, praying to the universe that Braxton doesn't hear me. The water is still running, so I think I'm good.

But my word...that felt so good to say out loud. So *right*.

My so-close-we're-sisters friends are dancing on the other end of the screen. Hate to bust their party but... "I'm in love with him, but I am doing absolutely *nothing* about it."

They freeze, rushing back to the screen and filling it with their concerned faces.

"And why the heck not?" Lucy snaps.

"I'm with her on this one," Lorelei says, raising her brow. How does that brow raise make me feel like a child who just got busted sneaking a cookie before supper time?

"He's my best friend. What if we don't work out? I'd lose him forever." There's no use in trying to keep my fears at bay with them now. "He is way too good for me."

"HADLEY ANNE DAWSON!" They shout at the same time. I cover my ears and look anywhere but the screen for a moment. When I finally direct my attention back to them, their faces are sharp arrows.

"Do not *ever* say that again," Lucy says, wagging a finger.

"He's a good man," Lorelei agrees, "but that doesn't mean you don't deserve him. You are a one-of-a-kind woman. He'd be lucky to have you." The water shuts off in the bathroom, and I bring my index finger to my lips.

"I'll text y'all later," I whisper. "Lucy, we need to talk about...*things*."

I hear them hollering for me to wait before I hang up.

I busy myself on my laptop on the small desk in the hotel room. I do need to check online sales and touch base with Karoline to see how the boutique is running. No doubt she is doing an awesome job as always. I have to admit, it's nice to be away from the store and the Tease Jewelry warehouse. Running your own boutique and jewelry line is a full-time, seven-days-a-week job. I can't recall a time since opening that I've had a vacation.

The bathroom door opens, and I command my eyes to remain glued to my emails on my laptop. The fresh scent of pine, moss, and a hint of lavender assaults my senses. *Don't inhale too deep, Hadley. Be cool.*

"Shower's free," Braxton says. Should I risk a glance? Surely he put clothes on before walking out. I decide to go for it.

I turn my head and bite my tongue.

He sports gray sweats, but that's it. A chiseled, very bare chest stares back at me.

I've seen him without a shirt plenty of times, but the view never fails to suckerpunch me, leaving me breathless. And knowing he just stepped out of the shower smelling so clean and earthy... A few water droplets still roll down his abs. I watch them streak down ab one, two, three, four, five, six...

"Hadley?" He raises an eyebrow, a smile tugging at the corner of his lips. I continue to stare, watching as he brings the towel in his hands to his onyx hair to dry it. His biceps bulge at the action, and I think I'm going to pass out.

Hunks of Hallmark, people. He is THAT attractive.

Coming back to my senses, I shut my laptop and hightail it into the humid bathroom.

Placing both hands on the sink after I shut the door behind me, I take deep, slow breaths. I stare at my flustered, pink complexion in the mirror, though it's still fogged from his shower. Why is he getting to me like this? I've known him for YEARS. He has always been attractive, kind, and my best friend. The one man in my corner. The one who showed me what a man is supposed to be—completely opposite of the revolving door of men Mama had. Including my father, whoever he is.

He has seen through every man I've dated. Including Cheater Dank Nose Daniel. Braxton warned me that something wasn't right. He told me to be careful.

And he was right, as usual.

Braxton has always been the man in my life. Consistent, steady, and strong. I mean, what other 15 year old boy would shed his jacket to cover up a girl's blood-stained pants?

A slow ache spreads across my stomach, and I curse under my breath. It's like thinking about it brought it on. No, I knew my period was coming, but couldn't it have waited until I got back home?

I wipe the makeup off my face, brush through my hair, undress, and step into the shower, hoping the heat of the water will bring a soothing calmness to my body and brain.

The pressurized stream does its magic, and in the clarity of the water that's hotter than hell itself, I realize something: my hormones are on overdrive. They are buzzing around in my body quicker than a hummingbird. That's why the thought of Braxton is making me feel things. Of course, I've always felt things, but not this intense. It's because of my period and that thought alone brings a tinge of relief to my worries.

It'll all pass in a few days, and I'll be back to normal. No more of these I'll-die-if-I-can't-make-you-mine feelings. No, sir. I'll be back to my regular he's-hot-but-I-can-control-myself feelings.

I take a long shower. Longer than my usual twenty minutes.

Knowing the source of my outrageous feelings, I am confident enough to shut the water off and begin my nightly routine.

I wrap the large towel around my body and tuck it securely at the top.

Shoot.

We only have one room, and this time, there is no upstairs or downstairs. And I can't sleep in my makeup or I'll have a massive breakout in the morning.

He's your best friend. And though you are in love with him, you can't hope for anything more despite what your hormones say, I tell myself through slow breaths. *He isn't going to judge you. He saw you the morning you left for this trip. It's okay.*

Feeling more at ease, I decide it's time to get dressed and then exit my little bathroom safe haven.

I look around for my clothes. Where are they?

Realization slaps me in the face, leaving my cheeks hot and burning: I forgot my clothes in my rush to the safety of a shirt-less-Braxton-free bathroom.

Taking a few steps to the door, I place my ear against it to listen for him. Turns out, it's a bit harder to hear from in here than out in the room. After a moment of concentration, I still don't hear him.

"Braxton!" I call his name out. No response. I yell his name two more times to no avail. I crack the door open just enough to stick my head out. He isn't in the room.

Wrapped snugly in my towel, I make a dash for my suitcase (remind me why I chose the far side of the room again?) and start digging for my pajamas. Once I've secured the package, I jet back to the bathroom. I have no idea when he will walk back in.

I dress hastily, then exit the bathroom for good.

I examine the room. My side is a mess, clothes are thrown haphazardly, which, to my defense, is a result of the clothing heist that took place moments ago. Braxton's side is organized, his shoes lined up by color against the wall. I sit down at the desk where I was working before Braxton interrupted me with his sexy shirt-less-ness. A note in his neat handwriting rests on my pink laptop. Why couldn't I have been blessed with the natural ability to write in script?

The note read: *Gone to the gym. Be back in an hour or so. -Brax.*

The downside to his handwriting is that a person needs a magnifying glass to read it. On another note, why in the world would Braxton go to the gym right after showering? A minuscule part of my brain hopes he went because he couldn't cope with the idea of me in the shower. That his brain broke the same way mine did while he was showering.

But that's just my menstrual flow talking.

I relax, knowing I have fifteen minutes to myself at the very least if he left right after I got into the shower. I contemplate texting Lorelei and Lucy back as I told them I would earlier, but I decide I want to settle into the large, cozy bed with an Agatha Christie read. I light the orange Pumpkin Pickin' candle that I brought from home that's sitting on the desk before falling into bed.

It's been a long day, and my body just wants to rest and forget about my confusing, enhanced feelings for Braxton, seeing Finley again as the stupid prince spilled my secrets, Mama and her issues, and lastly...Daniel. The man this whole road trip was planned around. I've done a great job of pretending I'm not hurting. It was only six months, after all. I blink away the tears pooling in my eyes before turning my brain off.

I crack open my book and lose myself in *The Mysterious Affair at Styles.*

CHAPTER SIXTEEN

BRAXTON

One last rep. I thrust the dumbbells above my head to complete the shoulder press, holding back a grunt. I'm not going to be *that* dude. I lower the weights to the floor, none too gently, then sit on the fitness bench next to me and slump over. I definitely pushed myself too hard tonight, but I had to make up for missing the past two days. Hadley still isn't telling me where we're headed next on this trip, so I have no clue if I'll have access to a gym.

Just the thought of her name stirs my stomach—and not in a good way. Not gonna lie, a smidge of guilt has been eating at me over all the flirting. I had put Hadley in a mental box and slapped a big red sign that read OFF LIMITS when I was younger. It was going well...until Mom passed away. It's like the void she left in my life was suddenly too large to ignore, and Hadley began to fill it in ways I didn't think anyone could.

"Hey, man." A voice emerges from behind me. "You finished with the bench?" I glance up to find a man around my age holding dumbbells of his own.

"Yeah, I'm done." I stand, stretching my arms out a little as I walk away.

"You okay?" The man has concern written across his face. *Bro, you're breaking gym etiquette.*

"Upper body's just tight," I remark, stretching my arms out again as if to prove my point. The man laughs and sits down on the bench, laying on his back and placing the dumbbells shoulder length apart.

"I wasn't talking about your workout," he muses in a deep southern accent. Not redneck Mississippi or slow Carolina, but maybe Tennessee? "You looked like you were sulking on that bench." He lifts the weights. Up, down. I continue to stare incredulously. *Gym. Etiquette.*

He finishes his set and sits up. "I'm a bit outspoken, so don't mind me. I know you don't know me, but we brothers gotta stick together when it comes to women." My body relaxes as if it knew before I did that I'd found a sense of camaraderie in this guy. I'll let gym etiquette go for now.

"She's my best friend," is all I say, and he nods his head empathetically.

"Friend-zoned?"

"No—yes," I huff. "Things have changed between us, and now she's got me on this romantic road trip that she'd planned for an ex before he cheated on her and she kicked him to the curb."

"That's tough, man." I laugh and nod along. The toughest.

"I'm always the designated friend." I feel a second wind coming on like I could max out on pushups again. "She needed a date for the homecoming dance? Me. A date to the skating rink? Me. Someone to go see the latest chick-flick with?"

"You," the man chimes in with a chuckle. "Does she have female friends?"

"She does, and they're great. But when she finds herself in need of a man on her arm, it's always me."

"The boyfriend without the benefits." He begins another set of dumbbell bench presses. A song by that very name begins to play in my head.

"What's your name, dude? We've gotten personal," I ask after a moment. He grunts—being *that* dude—before sitting up with heaving breaths.

"Mason Kane." He knowingly smiles. My heart stops.

"The country singer Mason Kane? The singer of 'Boyfriend Without Benefits'?" He stands up and extends a hand to me. I stare at it a moment too long before grasping it with a firm, excited shake. Is this what being starstruck feels like?

"That song's my new anthem." I still don't quite believe he is standing in front of me. Now I feel bad I didn't recognize him. "Dude, I'm sorry I didn't know who you were," I begin. "I don't make a habit of memorizing what singers look like. That'd be Hadley." Mason holds his hands up with little waves.

"No big deal. You're a guy. I'm assuming Hadley's the girl that's got your heart?"

"She's the one." I sigh. "The one waiting in the room right up that elevator."

"What are you doing down here with me then?"

"Burning off pent-up feelings." I laugh, feeling free and seen. Mason joins in.

"I know the feeling, obviously," he continues laughing. "I didn't catch your name. Where are you from?"

"Braxton Rawls," I say, wondering how in the world I ended up standing in a hotel gym in North Carolina giving my name to country artist Mason Kane. Should I ask him to sign my guitar? Nah. Mom gave it to me, and I'd rather keep it clean. "I come from the small town of Juniper Grove, Mississippi."

His eyes widen and recognition flicks across them. "Oh really? I'm fixing to build a vacation home there. Know any good contractors?"

I laugh. "Actually, my brother-in-law has a company. His name's Michael Kelly. He's been trying to get me to go back to school for an architect degree and join as the architect for the past few years."

"You design?"

"I play around with it, nothing serious. I work offshore for a living."

He grins. "My dad used to work offshore too. Say, you mind showing me something you've designed? Just to get ideas for my vacation home."

I pull my phone from my pocket and show him several projects Mom and I worked on together. Then, I show him my house that the architect of Michael's firm signed off on and I built.

"The interior isn't finished, but it's mostly little design things," I say, tucking my phone back into my pocket.

"A woman's touch is needed." Mason winks. "You've got real talent. Maybe you should consider joining your brother-in-law. Speaking of, can I get his number?"

I give it to him and direct him to Michael's website.

"If situations were different, maybe I'd consider it." Mom pops back into my mind alongside the memories of us building things together.

"Well, Braxton." Mason claps a hand on my shoulder. I hold in the wince at the soreness already setting in. "Don't make my mistake with the ladies. Go get your girl. Make her see you."

"Thanks, man." I reach out my hand, and he grasps mine one last time before I gather my water bottle and sweat towel.

I head back up to the room.

The one I'm sharing with Hadley.

Time moves at the pace of a sloth as I ride the elevator up to the room. My skin feels too sweaty. My mind is reeling over Mason's words: *Make her see you.*

Finally, in front of the room door, I swipe the key card before creaking the door open.

"You'll never guess who I met—" I pause mid-sentence as I see Hadley conked out on the bed with a book across her chest. After gently closing the door until I hear the soft click, I tiptoe to the left side of the bed where she's sprawled out. She looks peaceful, happy. I inhale a deep breath, catching the smell of her coconut shampoo. And is that...pumpkin, I smell? I look around the small room. The sight of a candle burning on the desk she'd claimed as her own earlier catches my attention. I stifle a laugh—the woman truly is *bougie* (her word, not mine). I blow the candle out, pretty sure they are not allowed in hotel rooms.

I shuffle as quietly as my six-three height will let me to the edge of the bed and slip the book out from under her arms. Agatha Christie...again. Hadley isn't much of a reader, but when it comes to Christie, she's read every book twice over. Pulling the comforter blanket up to her shoulders, I tuck her in. My hand travels to her hair. I pause, hovering right over the top of her head. Every inch of me wants to finger through her platinum strands, but I know if I do she'll bounce awake. I clench my hand into a fist before dropping it to my side.

Grabbing my pillow I had set on my side—I mean the right side—of the bed earlier, I ease onto the floor. It's not my side because we are *not* sharing that bed. I grab my blanket from my suitcase because unlike Hadley, I refuse to use hotel blankets and pillows. A prayer forms on my lips.

It starts silently, as most of my nightly prayers do. But at some point during my prayer, I begin speaking the words flowing from my heart.

"Lord, You see me. You know me better than I know myself. You know what I need, what I want. You know how desperately I want Hadley to see me as so much more than a friend. But she is Your creation. I know she doesn't know You yet, but I firmly believe and have faith that she will. In Your perfect timing. Until she surrenders to You, Lord, take me out of the way. I don't wanna be a hindrance, and I know I have been. All of that silly flirting, Lord. I can't seem to help myself around her. She is breathtaking. Not just her looks, though You surely blessed her there. But her soul. She is the most selfless, smart, kindhearted, caring woman that I know. She reminds me so much of my mom in those ways. Maybe that's why I feel extra attached to Hadley now. Either way, Lord, these feelings aren't going away. Bind my heart to You. Tune my heart to sing Your praise. Push me out of the way so that You can work in her life. One day, she'll be mine to cherish and hold. But until then, she needs You."

Teary-eyed and satisfied, I pull my blanket over me, and let sleep take over.

CHAPTER SEVENTEEN

HADLEY

He prayed for me.

I've fought tears back all morning while attempting to cover my face in make-up. I don't know why his prayer is getting to me so much. I haven't decided if I believe in God, but I know Braxton does. And the simple fact that he was willing to stay up last night in prayer over me... I take a piece of toilet paper tissue to my eyes again.

The moment he slipped the book from my hands, I woke up. I kept my breathing steady, though if I'm being honest, my heart rate picked up a tad knowing he was hovering over me. I'm the world's lightest sleeper, so I pretended to be asleep.

Why didn't I wake up to talk to him?

You can blame it on the dream I was in the middle of.

A dream that involved a shirtless Braxton, fresh out of the shower. Very similar to the experience earlier in the hotel room. Except in my dreamland, he kissed me.

And kissed me.

My face grows warm at the recollection of the dream.

So yeah, that's why I pretended to be asleep. I couldn't face the real man that I knew would be standing over me looking like a male model if I opened my eyes. I would have grabbed his face and planted one right on him.

I was almost asleep again—back to my sweet, dreamland kisses—when I heard him mumbling. His mumbling quickly turned to audible words, and I could tell his voice was shaky with tears.

My heart broke. Shattered into a million fractals.

He prayed for me.

Through tears, he prayed.

For me.

I still can't wrap my mind around it. His faith is strong, unlike that of so many others I see around me who claim to follow God. Braxton Rawls means what he says and lives his life in that way.

I would love to serve the God that Braxton does—to experience the constant joy that illuminates from him. Maybe life would feel a bit more meaningful. But that God has dealt me nothing but sour pickles in life.

Shaking off the myriad of emotions, I continue to apply my makeup. It's all just that time of the month, remember? Nothing to dwell too long on.

Besides, Braxton is in for a treat with our next stop on this road trip.

● 🖐 ✌

O r maybe I was the one in for a surprise.

     After our navigation app said there was a detour due to interstate repairs, we took a two-lane highway that led us to The Middle Of Nowhere, USA. To be completely honest, if we would have continued following the GPS, we would have been fine. We would have made it back onto the interstate.

But I am Hadley Dawson, and I am directionally challenged.

"Say it one more time." Braxton smirks with a tilt of his head, his arms folded across his chest showing way too much muscle to be legal underneath thin heather gray short sleeves.

"I am Hadley Dawson, and I am directionally challenged." I breathe the words as we stand on the side of the road with a slash in the front passenger tire from the cracked, unpaved road. The trees are thick, the sun waning, my phone is dead, and the road is a dead end. "We're going to be murdered here. So if you're done taunting me, I'd like to try and find a way back to society."

"I've called the closest mechanic shop I could find, Dawson. They said they'll be here in an hour."

"But wasn't that like an hour ago?" I complain. He shakes his head and turns on his heel. He's been pacing a trench in the already rubbled road.

"It was like two minutes ago." He stops, walks back to his truck, and lets the tailgate down. Then he grabs his guitar from the back seat and hops on the tailgate. As he props the mahogany guitar on his lap and begins to tune it, I forget I'm supposed to be worried about a sociopathic murderer looming in the thicket.

He plays a rhythmic melody that rises and falls like the seasons. A sound of rebirth, endless summers, falling leaves, and then joyous death after a life well-lived. My fears are locked away, trapped beneath the strums of his finger.

"What song is that?" I ask, not familiar with the tune. And I listen to a lot of music.

"Something new I'm working on."

"Am I the muse?" I twist my shoulders back and forth and flip my hair. I'm poking fun, but he stops mid-strum and looks at me with the hint of a smile. My antics reside as I get lost in his nature-green eyes. The sunset behind us does wonders to this man's eyes.

"You're always my muse," he says in a voice that reminds me of a wounded animal. I don't know what to do with that piece of information. Mostly because it felt way too real to be coming from the lips of my best friend.

"Wait. Shouldn't you have a spare tire?" I ask, redirecting the conversation. He lets out an exasperated laugh and the music stops.

"I should, shouldn't I? But someone never replaced it after she borrowed my truck and blew a tire out while I was offshore because her own car was down."

"I didn't know I was responsible for replacing it!"

"You weren't." He laughs. My eyes follow his hand as it splays against the body of the guitar. "But you were responsible for reminding me before this trip."

"I was planning to take my car," I mumble.

"But poor Hadley can't drive. She targets trash cans and innocent animals. And we can't forget she's directionally challenged."
His laughter is inviting, even through the insults. I find myself
chuckling along.

I mean, he's not wrong about any of it.

In the silence that follows, he begins to strum another song.
Another unfamiliar tune.

He sings about hearts and open spaces. It sounds like a love song,
but the way his eyes are closed and his chin is lifted towards the
sky, I realize it's one of his worship songs. This is usually the part
where I blow the popsicle stand, but I have nowhere to squirm off
to. The song is beautiful, especially the way it rolls off his tongue
in a low, slight rasp. My heart speeds up without permission.

"Did you write that?" I interrupt during a lull in the song. This
man could put me in a trance if I wasn't so diligent to remind
myself of who he is—MY BEST FRIEND. The perfect man. Too
perfect for me.

He continues to strum as he responds. "No. It's called 'Open
Space' by Housefires."

"It's beautiful," I choke out. He continues to sing, and I find
tears pricking the corners of my eyes. The words are penetrating. I
want to be open. I want to be open to true, honest love. I want to
be worthy of the type of love Braxton yearns to give. I want to be
open to God. I want to believe and to follow some power higher
than I am. So if I want it, why can't I? What's stopping me?

A roaring sound drags me from my thoughts. Headlights shine
on our concert for two, and Braxton sets his guitar down and hops
off the tailgate.

"Tank?" Braxton asks, walking up to the man who's sliding out of his truck.

"Yessir," the man says, then spits at the ground. His Carolina accent draws out slower than Mississippi. "I've gotta tire for you. Do you need me to put it on?" He looks from Braxton to me. The man's beady eyes plant on me with an easy smile. I finally get a good look at him, and my heart stops and my skin grows clammy. *No, no, no...it can't be.* He's greasy, and not just car grease. It's a vibe that radiates from him. One that screams: no good. One that I've encountered before. *You're in North Carolina. You are not in Mississippi. It's not him.* I repeat the mantra in my mind, though I can't shake off the fear gripping me with black tendrils.

I shrink back, folding my shoulders in, trying to make myself smaller and less desirable. It's not from a place of arrogance that I know I look good. Experiences through life and with men—one in particular who closely resembles the one in front of me—have told me that I am a desirable woman. But right now, I don't want to be her.

Braxton is suddenly beside me, wrapping a strong arm around my waist and hugging me close to him. Forget the independent woman gig. I welcome his safety.

"No, I think we can handle it. Thank you for the tire delivery. How much do I owe you?" Braxton stands strong and tall beside me. He radiates Protector, Defender, and Man.

The mechanic—Tank—gives Braxton a number. Braxton steps from my side and shields me from the front while he pays. The man sets the tire beside our vehicle. I never take my eyes off the unwelcome man. *It's not him.*

The fear doesn't fully release me from its grip until the man is so far down the road I can't hear his loud truck breaking through the silence of nature around us. Braxton, who stepped back to my side after the transaction, wraps me in a signature Braxton Bear Hug. His scent envelops me—a musky, wooded smell. It's a spicy-sweet combination that indicates home.

"I'm here, Hads. You're okay." His deep rumble showers comfort over me, and I let my muscles relax. I've never told Braxton about the man who took advantage of me in college. The one who kickstarted my twisted view of sex. I was so ashamed that I had let it happen. After growing up with the revolving door of men Mama kept around, you would have thought I knew how to spot a bad apple. But alcohol, late-night college parties, and the city don't mix well.

"Thank you," I mumble against his chest. With one last squeeze, I let him go. "Let's get out of here."

We change the tire together and get the heck out of that place.

CHAPTER EIGHTEEN

BRAXTON

We finally roll into the ski resort at dinner time. After lugging our bags up to *our* room—yes, another single room we have to share—we explore the resort hotel. My stomach is rumbling and the smell of steak is wafting from the kitchen and dining area, beckoning me like a siren. The way Hadley usually entices me. I can't even enjoy the fact that I'm going snowboarding tomorrow because of the intoxicating scent of steak. I hope there's potatoes.

"I'm starved," she says with a hand clutching her stomach. I nod my head emphatically in agreement, then lead the way to the dining area, keeping my pace just below a brisk jog. That detour and tire fiasco delayed us from Hadley's surprise destination, Alpine Ski Resort, in Raleigh.

"Flag down a waiter," I demand. She side-eyes me, but I'm too hungry to care. If Hangry Hadley is a monster, you don't want to know what Hangry Braxton is. I don't bother to check the menu. I want a medium-rare ribeye steak, potatoes, and broccoli. I tell the waiter as soon as he walks up. I'll have to apologize for my abruptness later, but food first.

"What's up with you?" Hadley asks. "You are like a ball of frustration right now."

"I'm ready for steak," I say. I'm pretty sure drool is forming in the corner of my mouth. I have half a mind to jump on top of the table and shout "feed me, woman," like Max from the movie *Where The Wild Things Are*.

"Ah, Hangry Braxton." She laughs. The waiter drops rolls on our table, in front of Hadley. With a wink, he's off. A sound between a growl and a snarl escapes my lips as if my body is instinctively reacting to a male hitting on my woman. Even though she isn't my woman. Yet. How many men am I going to have to fend off her this trip?

Hadley pushes the rolls towards me, pulling my glare from the waiter. "You first." I don't argue, but happily oblige.

We eat our rolls in silence. Both of us are too hungry to care about speaking anymore. After three rolls on my end, I sit back with a satisfied sigh. Well, I'm not completely satisfied, but enough to be civil again.

"You could've split that last one," Hadley says. The glint in her eyes tells me she's joking, but now I feel kind of bad I didn't offer.

"We can ask for more."

"Nah, I'm good. I'll wait for my own steak." As she says those words, the waiter appears with our food. My stomach and I are pleased at the quick service.

"I'll pray for us real quick." I make the statement politely to let her know I'm fixing to pray because I know she won't join me.

She usually eats through my prayers when I attempt them out loud with her.

"Okay," she says, tucking her head down like she's praying. What in the world? No mocking? No ignoring? But participating... *Thank you, God,* I silently offer praise. Then I lead us in a quick prayer.

We make haste diving into our food, conversation lagging in our efforts to shovel the food into our mouths.

"How's the steak?" I finally ask, finishing up my own. Broccoli and potato find their way into my mouth next. It's all heaven on my tongue.

"Not as good as yours, apparently," Hadley replies, drowning a chunk in A1 Sauce.

"Because you eat it burnt. That's not real steak."

"I'm not a vampire. I don't want a side of steak with my blood, *Edward.*"

Here we go with *Twilight.* I won't be surprised if I'm forced to watch that bad excuse for a movie tonight.

She speaks again before I can respond. "Oh, let's see if we can watch it tonight!" Great. I summoned her desire for the ridiculous movie. *Please God, no.*

"If you make me watch that movie one more time..." I threaten, dropping my fork onto my empty plate. I inhaled my food, and now my stomach is a balloon fixing to pop.

"What are you gonna do?" she challenges, fixating her eyes on mine and setting her own fork down. She crosses her arms and sets them on the table, leaning in.

"It's what *you* will have to do." I smirk. "Whatever I want for an entire day. Scrap your plans. Let me take the reins."

"Sounds harmless." Hadley's laugh has ideas reeling in my head. "We're watching *Twilight!*"

● ✋ ✌

"You know, I may actually enjoy the movie more if you would quit playing every single role." That's a lie. It's insanely adorable how she changes her voice for each character. Maybe I'd like the movie more if it was *Twilight: Hadley Dawson Stars in a One-Woman Show.*

"So, what's my punishment for making you watch this?"

I grin, turning my face to her. Mistake. We are too close sitting up in this single bed in a dark room. I swallow, then look away before answering. "You'll have to wait and find out. That's part of the deal."

"I love surprises, Brax," she says. "Did you forget that?"

"Sure didn't, Bully. But maybe this one'll make you regret that statement." I still haven't solidified my Braxton's Day yet. Yes, it has a name. And yes, it's written in my notebook waiting for bullet points to appear beneath the bolded words.

"Try me," she challenges. I dare to meet her eyes again. She has one eyebrow cocked up, and I want to take a finger to it and smooth it down. She turns her head back towards the movie. "Oh, I love this part!" The vampire guy steps into the sunlight and sparkles. Snorted laughter breaks through me, and she hits my arm. "Shh, you're ruining the moment!"

"How do you think I'd look if I unbuttoned my flannel and sparkled in the sunlight?" I question through my laughter. That pretty pink color lights her cheeks, reminding me of the lollipops Hadley so often eats. She hits me a few more times before breaking out in her own laughter.

"Fine, it's ridiculous," she admits through fits of laughter. After the day we both had, I think letting loose is exactly what we needed. She tumbles over in laughter, falling into my chest. I wrap my arms around her instinctively, pulling her close as we laugh. Though our laughter quickly dies down with that action.

"Thanks for coming with me, Brax."

Her head still rests against my chest, my arms holding her close to me as if I am never letting go. I don't want to let go. "I wouldn't have it any other way," I reassure her.

She sits up, and I unwillingly let her go.

"I felt like I kind of forced you into this," she says. I sit up straighter, turning to look her directly in the eyes.

"No, you didn't. I agreed to watch the movie. Besides, you gave me a day."

"No, not this." She gestures around the room. "This whole road trip."

"I was going to say yes the very moment you asked me," I say. "You never had to beg or fight me for it. I was all in." Pausing for a moment, I add, "I am all in."

"Okay," she whispers, turning her eyes away. She yawns, though I think it's fake. "Time for bed. You can sleep on the bed tonight. I'll take the floor."

"As long as you are rooming with me, you'll never take the floor."

Her attention snaps back to me as she stares, blinking as if she didn't quite understand my words. The silence is only filled by the ongoing movie.

"Thanks, Braxton," she says with a soft smile. Her skin is glowing in the shadowed room, and I realize...

"You're not wearing makeup."

She covers her face with her hands and drops her head towards her chest. "I don't make a habit of wearing it to sleep."

Wrapping my hands around hers, I peel them away from her face. Inch by inch, she lifts her beautiful eyes towards me.

"You should go natural like this more often. I like it." The television light dances off her bare face, and I find myself leaning in. Her eyes widen before she blinks and shifts away.

"Goodnight," she says. Her hands search around the bed until she lands on the remote. She clicks the television off.

"Goodnight, Hadley." *You'll be ready to kiss me soon enough,* I think to myself. I throw my legs over the side of the bed and make my pallet on the floor before heading to the bathroom to get ready for bed. You'd be surprised at how many ways you can avoid a person in a small, enclosed room.

Instead of sleep finding me, I lay on the floor gazing up through the darkness. I'm so close to spilling my soul to Hadley. How much I love her, want her, *need* her. I can't be misreading things. All the signs are there. She flirts with me, and I flirt back. Any accidental touch sends jolts through my body. And it's not just the physical. I've known I wanted to be with Hadley for a long time now. She's the light of my world. Her playfulness, feisty attitude, kind heart, and ambition quickly became my only requirements for a wife as we went through high school and entered college, but I knew she wasn't ready. I'm starting to think she may never be ready, at least in her own eyes, but I want to work through that with her. By my side. As her man.

"Braxton?" Hadley's quiet voice breaks through my thoughts.

"Yes?"

"I can't sleep. Could you play one of those worship songs? The one you played when we were stranded earlier?" Her voice cracks at the end of her request.

I'm stunned silent.

But I grab my guitar, sit in the chair across the room, and play, my movements illuminated by the night sky pouring in through the window.

CHAPTER NINETEEN

BRAXTON

How is a man supposed to concentrate on snowboarding when a woman like Hadley is wearing a perfectly tight base layer top? She shed the thick ski jacket after two rounds of lessons and now sports a pristine white, tight top that hugs *everything* and hot pink snow pants. Her platinum hair is braided down her back. Goodness, I can't look away though I know I need to.

I'm so tired of looking away.

But I've wanted to do this activity my entire life, so I have to look away if I want to make it down this mountain again. No distractions.

Inhaling a huge breath, the cold air cutting my throat, I thrust my hips in one solid motion like the coach taught me. I move, but not as much as I need to. There is still too much distance between the downward slope and me. I thrust my hips again, this time adding a little hop with my board. I'm at the edge of the slope, ready to descend into blissful, frigid snow. One more thrust and hop, then the wind licks my face as I race towards the bottom.

Snowboarding. Is. Epic.

I'm almost to the end of the Easy Way trail when I lean a little too far forward, causing my board to come out from underneath me, and making me fall flat on my face as my momentum continues to carry me across the icy snow.

Still epic. I'm proud to say that was the first time I've fallen so far.

"I can fall better than you," Hadley taunts me. I shake the snow off my face just in time to see Hadley skiing around me, body moving forward while she looks over her shoulder at me. She pizzas her skis to try and stop, but tumbles over them instead. The way her legs went over her head clearly shows that she very well can fall better than me. Her high-pitched wail brings me to my senses. I unlatch my board and trudge through the snow to her.

"Hadley!" I holler her name, mostly as a way to let her know I'm coming for her. I pick up my pace, collapsing beside her in the snow. "What hurts?"

"My wrist," she cries out. I put my arms around her and help her sit up, noticing she's holding her right wrist.

"Here, let me see it." I gently peel her hand away from her wrist. It doesn't look bruised or swollen, but that doesn't mean it won't be later. "Let's get you to a medic."

Hadley nods and tries to stand up, but her skis are still attached to her feet.

"Hold still," I tell her before reaching down and unclasping her skis from her boots.

"I can do it." She swats my hands away with her good hand. I ignore her and finish unclasping the latches before helping her up.

Then I pick up her skis, poles, and my snowboard, and we shuffle through the compacted icy snow to find medical personnel.

All while she protests my help.

"We made it through lessons and three times down the Easy Way." I laugh, shaking my head and ignoring her plea to let her carry her skis and poles. Hadley glares at me, but a smile breaks free of her pained expression. "Always an adventure with you, Hads."

"Oh, don't think an injured wrist is going to stop me," she comments as a woman walks in. "I'll be back on the slope showing you up in no time." I notice the red medical sign around the woman's bicep.

"I wouldn't be so sure about that," the woman says with a friendly grin. She walks up to Hadley and introduces herself as Doctor Lane. "So, tell me what happened."

"She was trying to prove she could fall better than me." I smirk. The doctor stifles a laugh while Hadley gives me a look that screams "I will kill you."

"Why on Earth would you try to fall better than your..." Doctor Lane trails off, looking between us.

"Friend." Hadley and I spit the word out at the same time and at the same hurried speed. Doctor Lane raises an eyebrow, but continues questioning Hadley about what happened. I listen as she recounts her fall, wincing a little when she tells how she landed on her wrist and heard a pop.

"You'll need to get an x-ray to know for sure, but I think it's a mild sprain," Doctor Lane says to Hadley. "I recommend going to the hospital in the city to be sure. In the meantime, no more skiing for you. You need to ice your wrist, take ibuprofen for the pain, and keep it wrapped until you can get a brace."

"But I paid for this," Hadley sighs.

"We can offer you a partial refund. Especially since it's so early in the day." Doctor Lane turns to look at me after fishing out a wrap from a bin. "Would you like to continue, or are you tapping out with her? I'll be on break soon." I don't miss the suggestive smile in her words. Heck, Hadley and I said we were just friends, so I can't blame her. She's got to be close to our age, and she's pretty—honey blonde hair pulled back in a ponytail, soft blue eyes, and a kind smile.

But I'm not the kind of man that would flirt with another woman just to make the love of my life jealous. I'm all in for Hadley, and I'm desperately trying to prove it even if I'm moving at a sloth's pace to respect her recent breakup.

"I need to be there to help her if she needs it," I say to the doctor while smiling at Hadley. Hadley, who had been scowling only moments ago, smiles back.

"Alright then," Dr. Lane says, still as kind as ever. "Let me wrap your wrist and then we'll get you two up to management."

Hadley

I 've been watching those videos where best friends kiss.

Some unaware guy gets one planted on him by his female best friend. Sometimes, I'm pretty sure it's all just a setup for internet clout. But there are some where the girl kisses him, ever so gently, and then his eyes clear as if he is finally seeing the world for the first time. That wasn't planned, nope. But their lives just changed forever.

I wonder if I could pull that on Braxton? Grown adults can do the trend, right? That way if he brushes me off, I can simply blame needing the views for my boutique. Karoline would eat it up.

But until I build up the willpower, guts, bravery, and all the other things to do *that*, I'll happily bask in the fact that Braxton chose me over the cute blonde doctor. When she invited him to go on the mountain with her on her break, my heart sank. And in that moment, I realized I never wanted to see Braxton with another woman ever again.

I'm in love with him.

He's a good-looking man with his onyx black hair, trimmed facial hair, dark emerald green eyes, plush and kissable lips...

Snap out of it, Hadley. But dang, he's fine. And seeing him with nothing but base layers on...*gulp!*

But it's not just his looks. I *know* Braxton. He is the man who would take in a stray cat despite being allergic. Everything he does, he puts his heart into it. He loves people, delights in serving others, and has always been there for me. When no one else was there, Braxton was. Even if I didn't necessarily want him there. He sang for me last night when memories of *that night* reemerged from the pit I had buried them in. He would love me wholeheartedly and with every fiber of his being. *I know it.* Can I accept that I'm possibly worthy of that love?

"How's the wrist?" Braxton asks, setting a cup of water beside the bed after handing me two ibuprofen. This simple act of caring has Salt-N-Pepa's "Whatta Man" playing over and over in my head.

"Aches, but nothing these pills won't fix." I wince at my words, thinking they sound a little too familiar. A little too much like Mama. *Chill, Hads, it's just ibuprofen.*

"You sure you're good?" Concern flashes in Braxton's face. I nod, picking up the water to wash the medicine down.

"Well, what do you want to do with the rest of our day?" I ask. I'm still bitter over not being able to stay on the mountain. It was unlike anything I have ever experienced. The sheer beauty of the world around me on that ski lift, with Braxton by my side, convinced me there was a Creator. There's no way that beauty just happened. But I still have questions. So many questions. Like how could a loving God let me be born into the messy situation of my mother? Or how could a God that supposedly had my best interest in mind allow me to fall victim to a horrible, soulless man who treated me like an object? Who allowed me to see a future with a good man for a split second before ripping it away? Well, at least I thought he was good. Maybe God really was looking out for me with Cheater Dank Nose Daniel.

"You need to rest, Hads," Braxton says, sitting down beside me on the bed. He's too close. He pushes all thoughts of my ex from my brain. *Gah,* it's suffocating how my stupid, hormonal body reacts to Braxton these days. And it's amazing how he makes me feel like I could enter into another relationship so soon.

I try to envision the scrawny kid I once knew in grade school, but nothing comes to mind. It's all man in front of me today. A kind and caring man, which makes him all the better looking in my eyes. "Besides, don't we have to get up early to head to Chesapeake for the wedding in the morning?"

"We do, but that doesn't mean we can't still have a fun day. My wrist is fine. I've taken the medicine, we went and got a brace from Walmart, and I *promise* it's not broken. I'd feel it," I plead. I'm incredibly thankful I talked him out of taking me to the hospital. Technically, he let me win our Rock, Paper, Scissors game, which allowed me to make the choice not to go. The hospital is the last place I want to be. "So, I'll ask you again. And if you don't answer, then I'll take it upon myself to pick something. What do you want to do?"

Braxton stiffens, his facial expression pained. What in the world? He swallows, his cheeks turning an attractive shade of pink. Isn't it something when you can make a man like Braxton Rawls blush? I don't know what I did or said to cause it though.

"Want to explore the town?" he finally asks.

"Why yes, I do," I say, already hopping out of the bed and heading for my luggage. I've been researching what there is to do around here on a Saturday afternoon and evening. I grab my cowgirl boots, ripped high-waisted skinny jeans, a tank top, and flannel. "Wear your boots, Rawls."

"I always wear boots..." he mumbles as I slip into the bathroom to get ready.

CHapter Twenty

HADLEY

George Strait's "Check Yes or No" floats from the building, and the smell of chicken wings infiltrates my senses. Lights hang across the outdoor porch where people are playing pool, dancing, eating, or all of the above at once. *Oh yes,* I think. *My kind of place.* I check my phone again, one last time, to make sure it has enough juice to get me through the night.

Because tonight is the night I kiss my best friend.

Of course, I'll be recording it in the name of the video challenge in case I've read him all wrong this entire time and need a cop-out as to why I assaulted his face with my cherry-red lips.

Yes, I chose cherry red lipstick to kiss my best friend.

Oh my gosh, I AM FIXING TO KISS MY BEST FRIEND!

My heart beats wildly out of my chest and my breathing becomes labored. I can't chicken out of this. It's time. I know I'm not good enough for him, but maybe...just maybe...that will be okay with him. I'm tired of waiting, of pining, of wishing and hoping. If he isn't going to make a move, I am more than happy to woman up and do it for him. Because I swear he's been flirting with me. There's no way I'm imagining it.

"You know I don't dance, Hadley." Braxton groans, walking up beside me. I didn't realize I had left him behind. Well, that's not a good start to the evening. "Besides, aren't you tired from walking around town all afternoon?"

Yes. "Nope, not at all," I say instead. I have plans, buddy. Big plans. "Let's go!" I take his hand and drag him into the country dance club.

We pay to enter, get our legal-to-drink wristbands though I don't plan on doing that, order wings, and seat ourselves at a table in the corner of the building. It's small inside and everyone is low-key and chill. The real party is happening outdoors on the large porch. I slide into the booth next to Braxton instead of sitting across from him. He gives me a funny look, but I shrug it off. Everything is *totally* normal. I glance around, wondering where I could sneakily hide my phone. Or maybe I could just be upfront and tell him I'm recording a social media video for my boutique's page and need his assistance for a part of it. My mind continues to contemplate the best course of action as the wings are delivered to the table.

Goodness, that was fast. I need to execute this before we eat because... Gross. I don't want to kiss him for the first time with honey barbecue breath.

"Hold up," I say as he pulls a basket of wings in front of him. I push the basket back, and his face falls like I took his favorite toy away. If he was a child, that is, which he absolutely is not. "I've got to record a little video for the boutique, documenting the journey and such," I lie.

"Need me to hold the phone?" What a trooper.

"Not this time. You need to be in it."

"Why?" he asks, narrowing his eyes in suspicion.

"It's a trend. Takes two people."

"Oh-kay," he drawls. "What do I need to do?" My heart is exploding. Right out of my chest. I'm pretty sure all that's left is the chest cavity where it once pumped.

"Just sit here until I look at you. When I look at you, turn your head toward me." Really? That's all I could come up with?

"Alright," he says with a skeptical lilt. But hey, at least he agreed. This is it.

My hands shake as I set my phone up on the top of the booth opposing us. I almost drop my phone from the mounting nerves, but thankfully, it stays right where I placed it.

My mind goes numb. Or is it so hyper aware that it's forgetting to process anything?

I press play, and the challenge tune "Electric Love" by BØRNS begins to play from the phone's speakers.

My hands are sweaty, so I quickly wipe them on my jeans. I can't breathe. My heart is beating way too fast, my vision clouds. I need to do this now...

Without another thought, I reach my uninjured hand to his chin and grab, pulling his face smack into mine.

The first mistake is grabbing his chin like I'm dangling off a cliff and holding on to the edge for my life.

The second mistake is kissing Braxton's very shocked, very open mouth while mine mirrored his.

Why is mine open in shock? I know about this attempted kiss!

Teeth clash against teeth and our noses smash against each other's cheeks. *Holy ouch!* I'm not sure who jerks away faster.

"Did you just try to kiss me?" Braxton asks incredulously, rubbing his nose before moving to his jaw.

Kill. Me. Now.

"It was a social media challenge," I blurt out. An embarrassed groan escapes my lips as I turn my face away from him. Someone please give me amnesia. It's time to forget this EVER happened. Oh my gosh, what was I thinking?!

Abort mission!

That was AWFUL.

I risk a glance his way, ready to apologize and make self-effacing jokes.

Braxton's blank expression sends my heart beating more wildly than before. What is he thinking?

"I'm sor—" I begin, but he interrupts.

"You didn't do it right." His husky voice, followed by a gutteral sound deep in his throat, sends shockwaves through my body like the time I accidentally touched an electric fence when sneaking onto private hunting land. He shakes his head with a huff of breath like he's in disbelief, trying to make sense of what just transpired. I mean, I am too. But then he slides his hands to cup my warm cheeks. His hold is firm, but gentle. Green eyes, a dark, dangerous color under the soft light, glisten into my own.

Then those eyes flick down to my lips.

He leans in.

The electric waves turn into tsunamis as his lips brush against mine, so much softer than I ever imagined or dreamed. His lips linger against mine, unmoving but savoring. Like the whole world stopped spinning to keep time still at this moment. Slower than when he moved in, he leans away.

I realize I kept my eyes open the entire time. *Good gracious.*

"Electric Love" continued to play from my phone speakers. What felt like an eternity was most likely only a few seconds.

My best friend just kissed me.

BRAXTON JUST KISSED ME.

His eyes lock with mine as we sit in silence, heavy breaths releasing the pent-up tension between us. His hands rest gently on my face, his forehead leaning against mine.

"Did we just...?" I ask, baffled THAT just happened. HE kissed ME.

And it was already the best kiss of my life.

"I'm going to do it again." He sighs into my parted lips. I close my eyes, giving him the green light to kiss me as much as he pleases. Shivers rake my body as his lips latch on to mine, hungry yet gentle. One hand travels away from my cheek and weaves into my hair while his other hand finds my waist, tugging my body closer. Even as we sit awkwardly in this booth, our bodies mesh together perfectly.

I deepen the kiss, completely lost in his essence. Years of love, desire, and happiness transfer from my lips to his. Can he feel how much I love him? My hands wrap around his neck, and I flinch when my braced wrist clashes with my good hand. Braxton notices and pulls away with labored breathing. *Curse it all,* I think, wishing we could all just forget my wrist was injured. But no, Braxton is a perfect gentleman who will always make sure I am okay before his own wants. *But you won't,* the self doubt inside me smirks. *You're too much like your mama.*

Shut up, I retaliate against the negative thoughts. It's time to put those types of thoughts in the trash can where they belong. Braxton's eyes are glazed over, mirroring my own I'm sure.

"Is your wrist okay?" he asks breathlessly.

"Yeah," I mumble.

"I've wanted to do that for a *very* long time." He turns his body forwards and slouches down into the booth like he just finished running a marathon and is exhausted.

"Me too." I mimic his actions. "And I got it all on camera." I risk a glance in his direction.

"Hadley Anne Dawson," he barks my full name as he straightens up in the booth to face me. "If you post that anywhere I will never put my lips on yours again."

"So, you're planning to do that some more?" I wiggle my eyebrows. Despite his threat, a smile stretches up to his ears. To be honest, I haven't seen Braxton this happy since before his mama passed away

"I'm planning to do that as long as you'll let me." His eyes hood over and it's the sexiest thing I've ever seen, melting me into a puddle at his feet.

"As much as I would love to sit here and kiss you the rest of the night, I had some other things in mind." I wink.

"Like what?"

I nod my head towards the outdoor porch.

"Dancing." He groans, but slides out of the booth and offers his hand to me. I take it as butterflies twirl and spin in my stomach. "Hey, what about the wings?"

My stomach growls, and I definitely want to eat them. But I want to dance with Braxton more.

"They'll be here after a few dances." He looks longingly at the chicken on the table, but then turns away and leads me toward the dance floor.

"Oh, hold on." I stop him before we get too far from the table. I pick up a napkin, wet it using the condensation gathered on the glass, and gently wipe my red lipstick from his mouth. "Couldn't have you going out there with my lipstick on your lips."

"It's a privilege to be marked by you." His smoldering eyes set me aflame.

I think I may very well be the happiest woman alive at this moment.

chapter twenty-one

BRAXTON

"You better delete that video," I whisper against Hadley's ear. "It recorded way more than I'm sure you were anticipating." I clutch her body tighter to mine as we sway back and forth to "Rumor" by Lee Brice. It's a fitting song, thinking of all the town's people back home in Juniper Grove. Every time they spotted Hadley and me together, which was often, a new rumor mill started that we were finally dating. And every time it would be false.

Until now, I hope.

Do we need to have that conversation, or does the way her braced hand is pressed flat against my back and the other fingering the hair stemming from my neck speak for us? And why does that little action of her fingers in my hair make me feel like I am the king of the world?

"It's a memory now," she says. "I can watch it over and over, reliving our first kiss."

Our first kiss. My heart speeds up at her words.

The moment her mouth crashed into mine—and yes, I do mean that first initial moment when she assaulted my face—I knew that would be my last first kiss.

"Watch you crash into my teeth over and over," I jest. She tugs at my hair, then pulls away from me. Or tries, I should say, because I don't let her.

My arms are a cage, and Hadley is the bird. She's never leaving if I have any say.

"I'll crop that out of the video." She smiles up at me. Happiness lights her face, reflecting my own feelings. Hadley kissed me. She's in my arms, dancing with me. I made her *this* happy.

I am the happiest man in the world right now.

The song slows to an end and is replaced with an all too familiar opening line: "Turn it up, boys."

The crowd roars and Hadley jumps backward, covering her mouth with her hands. "It's 'Honky Tonk Badonkadonk' by Trace Adkins!" she screams through her hands. "Dance with me!"

Do I tell her I actually know how to do this dance from years of Brandi and her friends line dancing at the house? I don't *like* dancing, but I *can*. In high school, when she dragged me to dances, I didn't dance because I was a too cool football player. The extent of our dancing was her hands on my shoulders, mine on her waist, swaying back and forth awkwardly like every other teen. When the beat ticked up, it was a mosh pit of jumping up and down and yelling the words to the song.

I err on the side of surprise, throwing my hands up and shaking my head, all while backing away to an open spot on the dance floor.

I take the first step forward and watch Hadley's eyes triple in size.

A crowd forms around me, everyone finding a place in typical line dance fashion. A redhead sidles up next to me, but before I can move away, Hadley is dancing her way between us.

My feet continue the physical dance, but my eyes emotionally dance with Hadley's as we move across the floor. We turn, and now she's behind me. The perfect time to put my own little twist into the dance.

I shake my hips as my feet move to the music, knowing all too well the reactions my sister's friends had when I finally got the hang of the dance and made it my own.

Hadley whistles behind me. "Looking good, Rawls."

We turn again, side by side. My eyes find hers, enjoying the flush on her face from the dance.

"Looking good yourself, Dawson." The smile that's been painted on her face since our kiss widens. She does a shimmy move, then throws me a wink. I grab her hand and lead her into a darker corner of the room.

"Let's continue that kiss from earlier," I growl, breathlessly. "I hate dancing." Her response is muffled as I take her face between my hands and draw her tinted red lips to my own.

Just like last time, my world explodes.

I've dreamed countless nights of kissing my best friend.

Reality is *so much* better.

W hen we arrive back at the ski resort hotel a little after midnight, we both collapse on the bed in a blissful state of exhaustion. We lay on our backs, side by side, nothing touching except our clasped hands. Every single spot where her hand intertwines with mine is on fire.

"It's been a long time since I've had that much fun," Hadley says. I turn my head to look at her and find that she's already looking at me. She wears the same wide smile she's held all night, and I still can't quite fathom that I'm the one who put it there. Literal dreams come true.

"Same here." I squeeze her hand. We continue to gaze at each other with stupid grins and dazed eyes for what feels like the shortest eternity before she gently pries her hand out of mine and sits up on the bed. I follow suit.

"I guess we should talk about..." I pause before saying the next word. A word I've wanted to say for a long time. "Us."

"There's an us, huh?" Hadley asks, laying her head on my shoulder. "I never thought it would happen. I didn't know you wanted me as a girlfriend."

She tenses, and I try not to laugh because I know she's embarrassed by the assumption that she's my girlfriend. "You're so much more than a girlfriend, Hadley. Like I said earlier, I've wanted to kiss you for a very long time." She relaxes, and I lean my head back against the headboard and close my eyes. I never want to leave this moment. "The timing was never right, it seemed."

Her breaths become ragged beside me in the silence of the dim room lit only by a bedside lamp. Then she sniffles and lifts her head from my shoulder.

"What's wrong, Hadley?" I lift up my head and turn my body to face her. She's smiling, though tears stream from her eyes. Loose hair sticks to her face, and I reach out my hand to tuck the strands behind her ears. She opens her eyes, the tears making the blue color glisten like the sun rising over the ocean water when I'm out on the rig.

"I'm just so," she sniffles again, bringing a hand up to wipe at falling tears, "happy."

I situate myself against the headboard again before pulling her close to my side. My arms fit so naturally around her like she was always meant to be the woman between them.

"Are we doing this?" I don't want to ask that question, but I have to. "Because I know you just got out of the relationship with the idiot of the century, and I don't want to rush you into—" Hadley cuts me off with her lips, and I forget what I needed to say.

She pulls away after a moment, slips her phone out of her pocket, and begins texting.

"What are you—" My phone vibrates with three beats, signifying a text from her. I take my phone from my back pocket as she grins up at me.

I read the text.

Bully: Ask me what the vibrations mean.

"What do the vibrations mean?"

She kisses me again instead of answering. Then, she whispers against my lips the words I've longed to hear from her. "I love you. Three vibration tones. Three words." My breath hitches, and I gently push her away to look into her eyes. "I've always loved you," she continues.

I search her eyes with my own, mimicking the REM stage of sleep. She's dead serious, and my heart swells.

"I love you too, Hadley. More than a friend," I whisper back, not bothering to hide the tears pricking at my eyes. I pull away as shivers charge through my body like the cavalry. "Now I've got to get out of this bed before I do something I'll regret." Her face falls, and I immediately hear the way those words just sounded to her. "Not that I don't want to, but I, well, you see, it's because I want to and I—"

"Shh, Rawls." She places a finger over my lips. I resist the urge to taste it. "I know what you mean."

Another shudder radiates through my body, and I throw myself to my feet. "Do you know how much I like it when you say my last name like that?" She wickedly grins and begins to repeat my name while I make my pallet on the floor. I don't know if I'm strong enough to do this...

"Hadley, I think it might be best if I see if they have a spare room for the night." I hope the hunger raging in my eyes is very clear as to the reason why.

She sighs. "You're right. We have to do this the right way. You're worth it."

I cross the room one last time, pull her into my arms, plant a kiss on her forehead, and say, "No, you're worth waiting for. Tonight was proof of that." Then I jog to the front desk, praying there is another room available.

CHAPTER TWENTY-TWO

HADLEY

I watch Braxton gather his things like a tornado leaving a path of cleanliness rather than chaos. He kisses me goodnight, then walks out of my room. I collapse on the bed, reveling in the fact that it still smells like him—earthy pine with a hint of spice.

A small part of me feels rejected. Men have *never* turned me down in the past. In fact, I've had to do most of the turning away. But logically, I understand why Braxton felt he needed to leave. If I was worthy of him, I would have been the one to suggest it in the first place. So maybe I'm not worthy of him, but I don't care anymore. He wants me, so I'm staying. I'll abide by his rules and wishes in the physical department as long as he still lets me have those delicious lips that I now know taste like a cool drink of water (yes, it's a taste. I'm fully familiar with it now).

We've crossed the friendship line.

It's sink or swim.

Do or die.

As Taylor Swift sings, it's going to be forever or flames.

And from where I'm at tonight, no matter the nagging voice in my head telling me that Braxton doesn't actually want me because he walked away, forever is looking mighty fine. Hadley Anne Rawls has a beautiful ring to it.

It's a visual clear as day: Braxton in the front yard teaching our sons how to throw a football. Me in the bathroom teaching our daughter how to apply makeup in a totally healthy way and not like Mama taught me. Family dinners around a round table. Stick figure drawings on the refrigerator. Closing my eyes in the arms of the person I love most in this world every single night.

The illusion shatters.

Braxton works offshore.

Which was one of the reasons I said we'd never work.

Again, I know with sound reason I can trust him. He is the epitome of a good, honest, loving man. In the twenty years I've known him—and somewhere along the way fell in love with him—he's never been NOT good to me. But will my brain allow me to rest in that knowledge, or will it constantly wonder if Braxton is remaining faithful when he's gone? Will thoughts of him leaving one day and never returning torture me for the months he's gone out of the year? Can I handle it?

"Shut up, brain. You're spiraling again," I chastise myself aloud. "He loves you. You've heard him say it even when he didn't know you were listening. He prayed for you."

And therein lies another issue: Braxton is a Christian, and I'm not. I've heard people talk about how Christians shouldn't date non-Christians. Will this be an issue for Braxton? Will he try to convert me?

Do I want to give this Christian thing a chance?

"Gah, shut up!" I slap a hand to my forehead. I don't have to think about this tonight. I allow memories from tonight to flood my anxious thoughts away. Thoughts of Braxton's lips on mine, his (totally surprising) dance moves, his megawatt smile, and his hands in mine like they were the missing piece to my puzzle. I swim in those memories as I head to the shower to wash the sweat from the long night of dancing off my skin.

The long night of dancing with my best friend.

My boyfriend.

● 👋 ✌

The pounding of the door jolts my body out of bed.

"Dawson, get up," an angry male's voice shouts from the other side of the door. I look at the time: six-thirty in the morning.

Shoot.

I rush to the door and fling it open to let Braxton in before I realize what I'm doing. He stares at me, eyes traveling from my hair I assume is sticking up like I was electrocuted, down to his t-shirt I stole out of his luggage while he was requesting a new room last night, and then to my bare legs and feet.

I slam the door in his face, thankful his shirt is big enough to hit mid-thigh.

"Hadley, what are you—"

"Just a sec!" I dash to the bathroom and take a brush through my knotted hair. The bra I left on the countertop after my shower last night will have to do.

"It's past time to go." Impatience plagues Braxton's voice outside the room.

"One more moment!" I secure my bra, wincing through the pain in my wrist, then throw his t-shirt back on. I dab a light coverage foundation on my face, pencil in my eyebrows, and swipe on a coat of mascara. I rush out of the bathroom to find pants. I sweep my eyes across the room I managed to destroy in the span of one night. Clothes hang from the chair in the corner of the room, one boot is halfway tucked underneath the bed, and I CAN'T FIND PANTS. *Why am I such a slob?*

"I'd prefer if you called yourself a beautiful, chaotic storm." I halt my search at his words from behind the door. I didn't realize I was talking aloud again. His words replay in my mind, sinking into my soul as I stand in the middle of the hotel room.

I finally take notice of a pair of jeans shoved between the bed and the nightstand. I have no clue how they got there other than in the midst of my unsuccessful wild search last night to decide what I wanted to wear today to the wedding venue.

The wedding.

Shoot.

I shove on the jeans and then open the door for Braxton to come in. He gives me another appraisal, this time wearing a tiny smirk, before leaning in to kiss me. Throwing a hand up to block his lips, I mutter, "I haven't brushed my teeth yet. You rushed me."

Braxton snorts and shakes his head. "You were supposed to be dressed, packed, and ready to leave by now. It's my fault. I should have known I would have to wake you up two hours early if we were going to leave on time." He removes my hand from in front of my face and plants a chaste kiss on my lips. How does that brief moment of contact cause 4th of July level fireworks to denotate in my body?

"You kept me out too late," I retort, already bolting to the bathroom to brush my teeth. I need more kisses.

"If I recall, it was your idea to go dancing," he says.

"But you had fun." My words come out stifled around my toothbrush.

"Only because you tried to knock my teeth out."

I glare at him. "You're never going to let me live that down, are you?"

"Not in this lifetime, babe."

Laughter explodes uncontrollably from me, and I spew toothpaste from my mouth all over the mirror and sink.

"You won't live that down, either," he muses.

But I'm too busy laughing to care. "Babe? You're going with *babe* as a pet name?"

"What? Too basic? How about pumpkin? You like that flavor and scent."

I wash my toothbrush off and rinse my mouth clean. "Doesn't mean I want to be called one." I wipe the sink and mirror down as best as I can without cleaning supplies before walking back into the room. Without warning, the scene happening around me knocks me senseless. Me brushing my teeth, Braxton laughing, light banter. THIS is happiness.

"How about a classic, like dear?" he asks.

"I'm not my grandmama." I laugh, wrapping my arms around Braxton. It's as natural as breathing. All the worries from last night have left the building. I want this forever.

"Then what would you like me to call you, Bully?" He looks down at me as I stare up at him.

"You already have several things you call me."

"But I want something special. Something that signifies *more*."

I bite my tongue, wondering if he will take the nickname as a shot against God. I say it anyway. "You can call me *Goddess Divine*."

"That's only for future special occasions." He winks.

"I can't believe you remember that." When was the last time we watched *Pride and Prejudice?* The Kiera Knightly and Matthew MacFayden version?

"Brandi's made me sit down and watch it with her, too," he says, then untangles me from his arms. "Alright. I want to kiss you, but first, you've got to get packed and ready to go."

"Aye, aye, Captain." I salute him before gathering my strewn-out belongings and shoving them into my suitcase. I slip on my black boots and tie his simple black shirt in the front. It's the fastest I've ever gotten ready. Mainly because I'm barely wearing makeup, and he doesn't seem to care.

"I love the way you wear my clothes," he says, coming up behind me and snaking his arms around me. He kisses my neck, and my body has a violent, visceral reaction. I turn in his arms, clutching his face with my hands. Pain radiates through my right wrist, and I hiss.

"I momentarily forgot about my stupid wrist."

"At least it's your right instead of your left," he offers. Yeah, I'm left-handed. And with that left hand, I draw his lips down to mine. A million lifetimes could pass, and I will never tire of kissing Braxton Rawls.

"Okay, we've really got to go if we are going to make it to Chesapeake by ten," he mumbles between light kisses.

"Mhmm." One, two, three more kisses. With a hefty sigh, I pull away. "Okay, let's go, *McDreamy*."

"Nope, not happening. Try again."

CHAPTER TWENTY-THREE

BRAXTON

R oad trips with Hadley are...spontaneous as is.

Road trips with Hadley as my girlfriend are leveled up.

Who knew equipping her with the power to caress my bicep with her fingertips when she wanted something would be so dangerous? That action alone is the reason we are pulling into the parking lot of the hotel in Chesapeake, Virginia an hour late. Hadley needed coffee before we took off. Then, she needed more only an hour into the drive. The coffee dehydrated her, so then she needed water. That's when the bathroom stops began.

And I gave in every time because of the feel of her soft fingertips tracing heart patterns on my bicep. I guess if I was smart I would have held off to see what more I could get out of her, as if I was a child on the playground tantalizing the pretty girl. *On the way home,* I think with a smirk.

"Wow, look at this place." Hadley's face is pressed against the passenger window, her chin fully in the air as she takes in the grandiose hotel seated on a hill with awe. I noticed it pulling in, and I can't disagree. The structure is fascinating, like a medieval castle but modernized. The gothic-style towers rise into the sky, and I wonder how many levels the hotel has. I also make a mental note to ask about the history of this place. I'm curious if it really was a castle. If not, I need to find out who the architect was. This place is a work of art. I wonder if I could design something similar but on a family of five scale?

A door shuts, snapping my attention back to my surroundings. Hadley's already out of the truck and reaching over to the truck bed to grab her suitcase. I jump out of the truck, grab my suitcase, and go to take hers from her hand.

She jerks away. "I can carry my own suitcase." Her words aren't snippy, just a statement, but they still cause my chivalrous side to ruffle.

"Doesn't mean you should have to," I say.

"Always the gentleman." She smiles up at me but still keeps her luggage in her left hand. "But I'd like to hold your hand while we walk inside if you don't mind."

I want to grab her free hand and make it disappear beneath my own. "Your wrist is sprained. I don't want to injure it further."

"Then just be gentle with me." She sighs, her eyes boring straight into my soul, and holds out her hand. Her words have a double meaning, I'm sure of it. The tune I've been writing with my guitar wafts across my brain. It's Hadley's song, and one day I'll show it to her. But I'm still working on the lyrics. Her words, "be gentle with me," begin forming a lyrical poem. I need to get inside and write it down.

I intertwine the petite fingers sticking out of the black brace with mine as if I am holding a withering flower, and we begin the uphill trek to the hotel—castle?—entrance.

Once inside, I immediately feel out of place. My flannel shirt, jeans, and work boots don't belong in a place like this. I begin to think it truly was once a castle, though did America have those? History wasn't my favorite, as I liked more hands-on subjects like wood shop. Hadley looks at ease, even though she is dressed more casually than usual. I still can't get over the sight of her wearing my t-shirt tied up at her belly button. It pairs well with her faded, distressed jeans and black boots. Look at me, noticing a woman's clothes. But then again, I always notice Hadley.

And now she's *mine*.

"Yo, bro? Who's got you smiling like that?" Hadley asks, bumping my arm.

"I am definitely *not* your bro."

"It's a video." She laughs. Of course. "But for real. What's up?"

"You're mine. After all these years, I somehow managed to win you over."

"You never had to win me over. I needed to be better for you." Her voice becomes a whisper by the end of her statement.

"All you need to be is you." I lean down and kiss her cheek. Pink blossoms in the space where my lips were.

"Okay, well, no need to confess our feelings here in the lobby. Let's go find—"

"Hadley!" A high-pitched woman's voice cuts Hadley off. The way she makes Hadley's name two drawn-out syllables lets me know we've just found Mary Anne, Hadley's old coworker, friend, and the reason we're here.

A short, curvy woman with wavy black hair bounds over to us, embracing Hadley in some weird dance hug as they jump and spin in each other's arms. A man, a few inches shorter than me, catches up and stands behind the women.

"You must be David." I hold out my hand. He shakes it firmly, a good sign. Mary Anne isn't a close friend of mine, but I've been around her enough because of Hadley to know the woman is sweeter than honey. We were all a little concerned when she announced her engagement to David Lawson, a man she met online and had only visited a handful of times due to him living and working in Virginia.

"That'd be me. The lucky man who gets to call this firecracker his for the rest of our lives." David's hand is still in mine, but his eyes are locked on Mary Anne, who has abandoned Hadley in favor of wrapping an arm around David's waist.

We release grips, and Hadley weaves her own arm through mine.

"Does that mean you're finally agreeing to set fireworks off after we say 'I do'?" Mary Anne asks.

"Guess you'll have to wait and see," David says, then turns to Hadley and me. "Can't tell her what my plans are after saying 'I do' because then she might not stick around. Got to keep a little mystery alive."

Mary Anne bounces on her toes. "I'm never leaving now, bud. You're stuck with me."

Hadley snickers at my side, which pulls Mary Anne's gaze away from David. Her eyes travel to our interlaced arms.

"Don't tell me..." she begins. I glance at Hadley, and she shrugs.

"Mary Anne. David. This is my *boyfriend*, Braxton Rawls." Hadley beams. The statement elicits another round of dancing, giggling hugs between the women.

"It's about dang time!" Mary Anne squeals. She releases Hadley and ropes me in for a hug. Thankfully, she doesn't bounce and spin. After letting me go, she grabs Hadley's unbraced hand and tugs her. "I need all the details. When? Where? Why? How?"

"Hold up, tiger." Hadley laughs. "I have to get my luggage that you're continually pulling me away from. Then I promise I'm all yours."

"Fine. But only because I know you have a new pair of jeans from your boutique in there for me, right?"

Hadley grins. "Of course. I couldn't show up empty-handed."

After grabbing her suitcase, she reaches on her tiptoes and offers a quick kiss that still manages to send electricity to my toes. Then the two ladies are off.

"Guess I'll show you where your room is," David says. "Then we can get a couple of drinks if you want." His expression tells me that he needs a moment away from the squeals and hugs too. A place of quiet.

"Sounds good, man." I follow after David, already liking this guy.

After tossing my luggage in my room (which again, makes me feel like I'm staying in the Royal Palace), I follow David out to the hotel bar. He's a man of few words, and I respect that already. With Hadley, I'm an open book. I can talk to her anytime, be in her presence anytime, and be completely comfortable.

But she's the only one outside of the immediate family I can be that way with. When I'm with other people for a length of time, I constantly find myself wishing I could crawl away. Big crowds, parties...weddings. Not my thing. My introverted brain howls at me to find alone space, a space where I can drag my guitar out, play a few chords, and chill.

"What're you having? It's on me," David says, taking a seat on the stool. He flags the bartender.

"Think it's too early for bourbon?"

"Not when there's a wedding in town," he laughs. "How do you take it?"

"Neat."

David orders two bourbons, neat. It'll be nice to have a drink since Hadley isn't around. I would never drink with her out of respect for her past.

"What made y'all choose this venue?" I ask.

"My family owns it," he says casually. Who is this guy? "It's falling into my hands when Dad retires from the business."

"And what business is that?"

"Hotel management." He takes a sip.

"Hotel? But this place looks more like a restored castle." I swipe a hand at our surroundings. David chuckles and shakes his head.

"It is."

"How in the world did your family come to own this? Were y'all the ones to restore it? Who did the contract work?" I fire off the questions as the man beside me takes another sip of his drink.

"Long story, but it was my grandpa who took over the place. He designed it to have more of a hotel feel, then he led the way on renovations. It fell into Dad's hands, and next, it'll be mine." He doesn't sound upset or happy, just...factual.

"Man, that's awesome. This place is a work of art." I examine the stone columns in the room and the supporting beams of the arched ceiling. "I'm almost finished building my cabin-styled house back in Mississippi. It started as dream designs, but then I decided I wanted to make it my forever home. Looking at this place makes me want to try to implement this design to a family home."

"Are you an architect?" David asks. I take a sip of my drink.

"No, I work offshore. Designing and building is something I do for fun when I'm home for my month off the rig."

He scratches his chin. "You seem pretty passionate about it. Why not make a career out of it?"

I laugh. "You sound like my brother-in-law. He's a contractor. Been trying for the past few years to get me to go back to school then into business with him."

"So what's stopping you?"

I swallow at the memories of Mom surfacing. "My mom was an architect. Before she passed away. We used to build things together all the time. She stirred the passion. By the time I made it to college, she was sick with cancer, and I needed a quick, good paying job to help support her medical bills." I stop for a moment, hoping

I'm not annoying the guy with my life story. He raises an eyebrow, prompting me to continue.

"Dad's a pastor, by the way. No money there." I chuckle. "Didn't have the time to get the schooling needed for a degree."

"Moms are awesome, aren't they?" He smiles. Somehow, it's the perfect response. Quite frankly, I'm tired of people telling me they are sorry for my loss. "What kind of cancer did she die from, if you don't mind me asking?"

I take another sip of my drink, letting the burn travel down my throat. "Carcinoid. It was a slow, grueling sickness."

"My older sister, Jane, died from leukemia when she was only twelve. I was seven at the time, and didn't understand what was happening. But my mom, she was always there. Even when Jane flew from this earth, Mom stayed strong while Dad fell apart."

"Moms are awesome," I repeat his earlier sentiment. Brandi comes to mind, and I don't let myself imagine losing her. I hold up my glass. "To Moms and sisters."

"Moms and sisters." He clinks his glass against mine.

We settle into an easy conversation, and I'm glad Mary Anne is marrying this man.

I need more guy friends.

CHAPTER TWENTY-FOUR

HADLEY

"Tell. Me. Everything." Mary Anne slaps my thigh with every enunciation. We plop down on the king size bed in my hotel room (this place is bougie) and I tell her everything.

I tell her of Cheater Dank Nose Daniel, needing a date to her wedding, and how I am desperately trying to overcome the internal critic living within my mind telling me I'm not good enough for Braxton.

"I always knew you two would come to your senses." She snickers, pulling me into a much-needed hug. Talking about everything that's happened over the past six days was a bit overwhelming. Did I rush into things with Braxton? He wasn't wrong. I was just cheated on.

I pull out of her embrace. "We admitted we've always loved each other. So that's something." I sigh, tapping my good hand against my thigh. "I hate this self-doubt. One moment I'm perfectly at peace, and then the next, the feelings of inferiority set in. It's so," I shake my head with a huff, "unbelievably frustrating."

Mary Anne thinks for a moment. "You're Braxton and Hadley. I mean, he knows everything about you, right? And he loves you. Let the peace win." My mind transports me back to college and the night that changed me forever. I turn my head away from Mary Anne. She knows about it. As do Lorelei and Lucy.

"You didn't tell him?" she asks, but it's more like a statement.

"No," I grapple for words. "I haven't told him. It's just... What if he looks at me differently? What if he doesn't want to be with me? What if he—"

"He's been with you practically y'all's entire life," she interrupts.

"I mean *with* me. Not only am I ruined from that night, but also all the times after that. You know I'm not a saint, Mary Anne." I unstrap and restrap the velcro on my brace. The unwanted memories swim around like sharks smelling blood in the water, poised to attack. "I don't think I can risk telling him. He may decide he doesn't love me anymore."

"Hads, don't take this the wrong way. You know I adore you." She places a hand on top of my good one. "You and Braxton make sense. He brings out the best in you. You bring out the fun in him. You work. And there is so much love between you two—a deep, rooted, unwavering love."

"How would I take that the wrong way?" I laugh, trying to mask the tears threatening to fall.

"I'm not finished." Her brown eyes hold mine. "He's the one for you. Always has been. You can't go into this relationship with him—one that is destined to end with you walking down the aisle and taking his last name—living a lie. He knows your past to a certain extent. Telling him about that night in college is not going to chase him away."

Several moments of silence, interrupted only by small puffs of breath, go by. I chew on her words, wondering if she's right. Am I destined to be his forever? I said I made that choice before leaving the ski resort, but did I actually mean it? Can I do this?

"I'll think about it." It's the only assurance I can give her. "But right now, we need to focus on YOU. It's your wedding! Rehearsals are tonight." I jump off the bed, throw my hands in the air as if releasing the negative thoughts into the wild, and twirl around. Mary Anne immediately joins me, and we giggle like school girls discussing their crushes as she tells me all about her time in Virginia these past two weeks with David and preparing their future home.

I can feel his presence behind me, as if some invisible force is drawing us together in the ballroom of the hotel.

"You look beautiful." Those three simple words, ruggedly flowing from the mouth of the man I am in love with and tickling my ears, make my knees weak. I never thought I'd be a woman who'd cave to the cliché of weak knees, but here we are—full force wobbling. If I move, I'll collapse like the London bridge of the childhood nursery rhyme.

Strong arms wrap around my waist, pulling me flat against my favorite person. With his arms acting as life support (because seriously, my legs are mush), I twist around so that I'm facing Braxton. He wears a satisfied smirk that says "I've got you right where I want you and you're not going anywhere." I'm okay with that, yes, sir.

"You're okay with what?" he questions. Man, I've got to stop thinking out loud.

I decide to be honest in my reply. "Being in your arms." At least that's one thing I'm being honest about...

"Good. Because I don't plan on letting go anytime soon." Yep. I read him like I read my own mind. I guess that's what we get for being best friends as long as we have before becoming more.

"Let me get a look at you. It's rare I get to see you all fancied up." I wiggle out of his arms, albeit begrudgingly, completely satisfied with the eye candy in front of me. Braxton wears a fitted navy suit that looks like it was tailored specifically for him. Every tuck, hem line, and fold of the suit kisses his body. I let out a whistle of approval, tugging on the lapels.

"What's a girl gotta do to get you to wear this suit all the time?"

"Marry me." My heart shutters to a stop. One missing beat, two missing beats, three missing beats, four..."Hadley, breathe." Braxton's concerned voice and hand pressed against the bare skin revealed through the cutout of my dress act as voltage to my stopped heart.

Breath fills my lungs like shoppers entering my boutique on Black Friday.

"I'm sorry. *Marry* you?" I blurt out in disbelief.

"Or not," he mumbles as he takes a few steps away from me, looking down at his polished brown loafers.

"You're not wearing boots," I state. "If you weren't wearing sneakers for the gym, football cleats, or in your bare feet, you were always wearing boots." I scrounge my memories, trying to recall one instance where Braxton wasn't wearing his boots besides the previously mentioned occasions. There are none. He wore his dang boots to prom. To homecoming. To the bowling alley (he had sweet-talked the elderly lady into not putting on clown shoes like the rest of us).

"I wanted to look nice for you." Braxton is still looking down at his shoes, hands slipped into his pockets, as I take a step closer to him.

"But you must've gotten this outfit before we left." Realization hits me like an eighteen-wheeler going full speed on the interstate. "You hoped to win me over on this trip, huh?" With my good hand, I take one of his out of his pocket and into my own.

"Guilty," he says sheepishly, still looking down, though a hint of color flushes his face. Shy is a good look on him.

"Why do you want to marry me?" I ask. His startling green eyes flick to meet my tilted stare.

"Should I quote *Sweet Home Alabama*, or...?" I cut him off with a kiss. Chaste, since we are standing in the ballroom of the hotel that is being used as the wedding venue with a bunch of people. "Not," he finishes with a grin.

"Hadley, I need you for the bridesmaid lineup!" the wedding coordinator bellows over the intercom system. Seriously, this place is too rich for its own good.

"This talk isn't over." I give Braxton a little love tap on his behind. Nothing he wasn't used to from his football days.

He shakes his head, the smile growing across his face. "I never said I was kidding, you know."

I heard that loud and clear, Braxton. You were, in fact, quite serious about me marrying you. But you have no idea what I've been hiding from you the past eight years of my life.

Chapter Twenty-Five

BRAXTON

W hy did I think it was a good idea to blurt out *that* question, or rather statement, to be honest, at this moment? *Stupid.* But I can't back out of it now. Not that I want to, but there were so many other ways I wanted to ask, could have asked, for her hand. She was just there, looking like an angel in her modest pale pink dress that had a sliver of ivory skin peeking out from the small cutout in the back. Just enough to reduce a man's mind to caveman status.

And apparently forget all sense of propriety.

I asked Hadley to marry me in the middle of one of her good friend's wedding rehearsal.

You're a real winner, Braxton.

Hadley was called away to do the actual rehearsing part of the night, saving me from anymore idiotic talk. Though I need to be clear and upfront with her: I do intend to marry this woman. Sooner rather than later. She's mine to love now, and God knows I'm not letting go.

"Braxton?" a familiar woman's voice calls, jolting me from my thoughts. "Braxton Rawls?" I turn around to find the person associated with the voice and see my old college girlfriend, the one who almost made me forget about my romantic love for Hadley.

Almost.

"Katie Bloom, what are you doing here?" I walk the short distance to her, joining the petite blonde woman at her table. She had several qualities that reminded me of Hadley, which is probably why I assumed I could have Katie if I couldn't have Hadley back in college.

"It's Katie Williams now. My husband," she points to the man standing front and center of the makeshift aisle, "is officiating the wedding."

"So, you did end up marrying a pastor." I chuckle, recalling the beginning of our friendship when she told me she wanted to be a pastor's wife. I had momentarily forgotten she was from Virginia.

"I always knew it was my calling." Katie laughs along with me. "Greg and I actually met the summer after you and I broke up. God's timing is perfect."

"That it is," I muse, thinking of how Hadley and I finally came together. I don't know why we had to wait so long, other than we both needed time to figure things out for ourselves. But will she say yes to my proposal?

"Who are you here with?" Katie's question pulls me from my thoughts.

I point to the breathtaking woman who is giggling beside another one of the bridesmaids. It amazes me how quickly Hadley finds a friend. "Hadley Dawson. She's Mary Anne's maid of honor."

"Ah, the girl you used to always talk about in college." A knowing look crosses Katie's features. "After we broke up, I had my suspicions about her being the reason."

"She wasn't the reason, Kat. You know that," I say, using her nickname from college. "It was a mutual thing, right?"

She sighs heavily before looking away. "Yes, it was. But mostly because I had my suspicions about the female best friend you never brought around." She cuts her eyes back towards me, a sly smile playing on her lips.

"Wait. You thought I was making her up?"

"You never showed me any pictures or introduced us to each other. You'd walk away anytime she called." Katie shrugs, and I burst out laughing. A little too loud as people around us throw dirty looks our way. Hadley, as if in tune to my laugh from halfway across the ballroom, looks at me.

Then looks at Katie.

I can't see Hadley's eyes right now, but if I could, I would bet a million dollars that they are burning with the hot fires of hell. She excuses herself from her female companion and walks with determined purpose towards me and my current female companion.

"Brace yourself, Kat," I whisper out of the corner of my mouth. She gives a slight nod before placing her hand on the table with her wedding ring angled up. Smart woman.

Hadley arrives at the table in record time for a woman wearing four inch heels. She sidles up next to me, draping an arm across my shoulder.

"Hey, *McSteamy*," she whispers into my ear, though loud enough for Katie to hear.

"Not happening either." I laugh and wrap an arm around her waist, loving the slight contact with skin on her back. "Hadley, this is Katie Williams. Katie, Hadley Dawson, my girlfriend."

"Ah, Katie from college," Hadley says, reaching out her non-injured hand to Katie. They shake hands politely, though Hadley's eyes remain intensely focused on Katie. I stifle a laugh. Feisty Hadley is a force to be reckoned with. Not that I don't mind the attention it's earning me one bit. But I never was the kind of guy to use another woman to make someone jealous. And that isn't starting now.

"Katie is married to the pastor officiating the wedding." Hadley physically relaxes against me and a genuine smile replaces the fake one she had plastered on.

"It's nice to meet you," Hadley politely says.

"Likewise," Katie replies. "I heard so much about you in college. But I have to be honest, Braxton here never brought you around so I thought he was making you up." Hadley laughs, but then it dwindles out.

"You guys dated your last semester, huh, Brax?" I don't know why Hadley wants to talk about this, but I answer with a nod. She continues, "That's right. I was just entering my first semester at that time."

Hadley almost looks like she could vomit at any moment.

"Hads, you okay?" I ask. She shakes her head before jetting off in her high heels towards the restroom.

"I better go check on her," I tell Katie.

"Let me. You can't go into the woman's bathroom." Valid point.

We make our way to the restrooms and Katie slips in after Hadley. I can't tell if she is throwing up or not because of the noise in the ballroom, but I pray to God that she's okay.

I make myself useful and grab a glass of water for Hadley.

"I t's too late for that bug to be catching up with you now," I say as I press a cold rag to Hadley's forehead. I'm sitting on the couch in her room as her head rests in my lap and the rest of her body splays across the length of the sofa. We're both still dressed to the nines in our wedding rehearsal outfits. When Katie emerged from the bathroom, barely holding Hadley up around the waist, I knew she wasn't okay. I informed David and Mary Anne that Hadley had taken ill. Then I carried her up to the room.

Hadley was a do-it-yourself woman. Miss Independent to a tee. The fact that she was draped across an ex-girlfriend of mine, no matter the fact the woman was now happily married, told me everything I needed to know: Hadley was far from okay.

She twists her head back and forth in my lap continuously like she can't find a comfortable spot to rest. The rapid movement makes it hard for me to keep the damp, cool rag pressed close against her heated face.

"No, please don't." She swats my hand away. Her eyes are glassy, somewhere far away.

"Hadley, it's me. It's your Brax," I slowly whisper each word as her thrashing about grows. Her arms fling about wildly, and she begins kicking her legs. Hard. "Hadley, baby. It's okay. I've got you. Everything's okay." I remove her head from my lap and evacuate the couch as she fights the air. Each whimpered "no, please don't" from her lips is like a blade to my chest.

I can only assume something from her past has come back to haunt her with an ugly vengeance. She has a myriad of horrid experiences with her mother.

Lifting her up, taking every punch, slap, and kick, I fold her into my arms. I squeeze as tightly as I imagine a boa constrictor would before sitting back down on the couch with Hadley curled in my arms. Her arms are locked down under my own, but her legs, still free, continue to kick as she whimpers. After several minutes, Hadley stills. An exhausted breath escapes her lips and she sinks fully into my embrace.

"Braxton," she chokes out my name through tears. When did she start crying? "I'm so sorry, Braxton. I'm so sorry. I'm—"

"Shh." I cut her off as I run my fingers through her loose platinum waves. "There's nothing to be sorry for." The question is burning in my throat—what the heck was that? But now is not the time to ask. I hold her, solid and steady as a rock, until she drifts off to sleep in my arms.

CHAPTER TWENTY-SIX

HADLEY

The pounding in my head jolts me out of a restless sleep. Though I don't remember making it to my room last night, I do remember Braxton holding me, telling me everything was okay. Telling me he had me.

Why now? Why did talking so briefly about college trigger the PTSD? I wipe the crust from my eyelids and attempt to sit up. The pounding in my head increases to that of a jackhammer breaking up concrete. Finally making it to an upright position with cleared vision, I notice Braxton asleep on the sofa in my room. My heart swells at the sight of him. Just knowing he spent the night in my room has my stomach rumbling.

No, wait. I never made it to dinner after the rehearsal. Heck, I never *finished* the rehearsal. *Oh gosh,* I groan inwardly. Mary Anne is going to kill me.

As if sensing I'm awake, Braxton stirs on the couch, his eyes opening and taking me in. He jumps off the couch and races to my bedside, where he picks up a glass of water sitting on the nightstand.

"Good morning, love," he whispers, using one hand to tuck loose hair behind my ear and offering the glass of water with the other. I gladly take the drink because if I try to open my mouth to talk, a tumbleweed might roll out. After a few sips, I feel confident enough to speak.

"I'm so sorry about last night," I say, tucking my head into my hands. The velcro from the brace on my right wrist scratches my face and then lodges into my hair. When I go to pick it out my face, it pulls. *Just my luck.*

Braxton reaches for the tangled mess of hair stuck to the velcro, but I shoo him away.

"I've got it," I say, but he continues to reach. I slap his hand away. "I said I got it!"

He retreats his hand, but continues to hover over me like I'm that ding in a windshield that will grow if not treated gently and with loads of care. I don't know why I'm acting like this towards him after his help last night, but it's like I can't stop. I was happy to see him here this morning. But now...

I'm just so angry.

At life. At *him*. At my mama. At the so-called God Braxton loves to worship.

"Just go away for now, please." I breathe carefully through each word. "I need a minute to be alone."

"Hadley, you don't have to—"

"Please," I bite. *Don't make me be harsh, Braxton. Please don't.*

He catches on and slowly disappears through the double doors of my hotel room.

Somehow, more tears manage to formulate in my eyes. They travel down my face silently, unlike the racking sobs I experienced last night. The salty liquid makes its way onto my lips and into my mouth. Lying back down on the bed, I let them fall.

I don't know how long I've repressed those memories of my freshman year. The party, the drinking, the guy who took everything away from me on that dirty bathroom floor. Something I had secretly hoped (and only admitted to my journal) to give to Braxton one day, should we ever find our way to being more than friends.

Tears fall until my eyes can't possibly produce anymore. I remember it all.

Broken. Used. Discarded. No good.

Those words became the mantra repeating in my head. The only way I knew to cope was to turn to drinking. And more men. This time, ones that I chose.

I became my mother for a short season of life.

When Lucy and Lorelei pushed me to start therapy, I listened. That got me out of the drinking habit, but not the other thing.

I gave myself away, time after time. After a couple of years, I stopped. Then Daniel came along, and I gave myself to him because I thought he would be the one. The universe only knew I would never be good enough for Braxton by that point.

Broken. Used. Discarded. No good.

But he loves you anyway, a voice inside my head whispers. It's faint, and I'm not exactly sure where it's coming from because I've never been known to speak too kindly to myself.

The voice isn't wrong. Braxton knows my past, though admittedly not the cause of my downward spiral through college, and he still wanted me. Wants me. Loves me.

Yet here I am pushing him away. What in the world is wrong with me? Why am I so messed up? Why can't I just accept the love he wants to give me?

Against my inner critic countering every small, positive whisper from somewhere else inside my mind, and against the pounding of my head, I throw on sweats and t-shirt, tie my hair into a knot on top of my head, brush my teeth, and run to Braxton's room, hoping...praying...he's there.

My heart races with each step towards his room. I make it, finally, and take a moment to place my hands on my knees as I try to catch my breath.

Before I can knock, his door opens. I stare into his stunned expression, then I throw myself on him, allowing more salty tears to escape from my eyes.

"Hadley, what's wrong?" Braxton's voice isn't right. It's missing the softness and concern usually laced in words like that. In fact, I'm holding onto him. His arms are at his sides instead of around me.

Did I ruin things between us before they could ever truly begin?

"In college, my freshman year," I begin. My only hope of a future with Braxton is to tell him the truth. He deserves to know, like Mary Anne told me. "I was at a party, and I think someone slipped something into my drink." The words come out stuttered through tears and sniffles. "I was...I was..." I try, but I can't say the word.

Braxton's arms wrap around me, one snaking around my waist and the other firmly resting against the back of my head. He holds me tight against him.

"You don't have to finish." His voice sounds splintered and ice cold. The voice I never wanted to hear nor be the cause of creating. But I had to tell him. Mary Anne was right. He holds me so tightly against him that I can't move. When he finally lets go, I meet his burning eyes, so opposite of his chilling voice moments ago.

"I'm sorry," I say. Those are the only words I know to say.

"Never," his voice warns, "be sorry."

I shouldn't ask the question, but it's dying to escape. "Do you still want to be with me?"

To my surprise, Braxton laughs. Not a boisterous sound, but a soft, unbelieving sound. He takes my face between his hands and holds it there as he searches my eyes with his own.

"Hadley Anne Dawson. You are the only woman I've ever truly wanted. Nothing, *nothing*, could ever make me want you any less. Love you any less. Do you hear me, you crazy, beautiful woman? Do you understand?"

With a single gulp and a nod, I let him claim my lips.

CHapter twenty-seven

BRAXTON

B ank on this: if I ever find the name of the sick, sorry excuse of a man who did that to Hadley all those years ago, when she was only eighteen, you can believe I'll kill him. I don't care that I'll go to jail.

I clench my fists at my side, willing myself to calm down. Hadley has been with Mary Anne for the majority of the day prepping for the wedding that starts in—I check my watch—fifteen minutes. And while she's been with the bride, I've been brainstorming a million different ways to become a murderer.

It's not healthy, I know. But I feel so helpless. I breathe out a heavy groan as I sit back in my seat waiting for the wedding to begin. A few people give me concerned looks, but I ignore them.

Why didn't she tell me sooner? How did I not see it? Sure, I noticed when she had changed and began going down a dark road during her freshman year, but I didn't think *that* was be the triggering factor. I simply thought she'd finally caved to the stress that had been weighing on her shoulders for her entire life. I didn't blame her, though I did try to stop her. It never worked, and she accused me of trying to save her as always. That's when I had Lucy and Lorelei step in, and it helped. At least partially.

But I guess that's reality.

I can't save her. I've never been able to, no matter how hard I try or want to.

Only God can do the saving.

Silently, I cry out to Him. I beg Him to reach her, to wrap her in His peace and comfort. To reveal Himself to her.

I love her so dang much it hurts.

Please, God. Please. Heal her. Do what only You can do.

An instrumental song begins to play, pulling me from my silent prayers, and I notice the pastor and David are at the altar.

The families of the bride, then the groom, are ushered down the aisle lined with rustic colored flowers. Next, the bridesmaids walk down the aisle.

My breath hitches at the sight of Hadley in the burgundy gown. It matches her signature lipstick perfectly. The top is modest, though sleeveless. It ties around her neck, sporting an open back from midway up. Her platinum hair is pinned into a low bun with curls sticking out in all the right places. As she passes me, our eyes catch briefly. I mouth "I love you," earning an award-winning smile from her red lips.

I stare at her the entire wedding. Our eyes meet again and again, each time eliciting a soft blush across her cheeks and a small smile that she tries (but fails) to hide. I don't hear the pastor, the vows, or the "I dos" at the end. All I see is Hadley. All I hear is the sound of our future unfolding before us.

I want this. Need this.

And I think I now know just how to properly propose to my best friend.

$$\bullet \text{ } \text{✌} \text{ } \text{☝}$$

Pulling Hadley onto the dance floor of the ballroom (the venue was immediately transformed after the wedding to host the reception), I begin to show off my formal dancing skills. Granted, they aren't as good as my line dancing, but I can lead and spin a woman around the dance floor. Especially when that woman is Hadley, who has had some classical training (thanks to her grandmama).

"Have I told you how beautiful you look tonight?" I whisper to her as I tug her against my chest as the song slows.

She giggles. "Only a thousand times."

"What about how much I love you?"

"Hmm, I guess I could stand to hear that some more." Her fingers fiddle with the hair at my neckline. This must be a habit of hers while dancing, but I sure ain't complaining.

"I love you," I whisper against her ear once more. "I love you." I kiss the space behind her earlobe. "I love you." My mouth finds her jawline. "I love you." A kiss on the nose. "I love you." A feather of a kiss on her red lips.

"Time for the bouquet toss! All unmarried women to the floor please," the DJ announces. Mary Anne dances to the center of the floor with her bouquet in her hand.

"Go get 'em, Bully." I shove Hadley away from me and towards the ever-growing swarm of women. I didn't realize how many single women were here tonight. Maybe it wouldn't have been as taboo as Hadley thought for her to come alone.

Though I regret nothing.

Mary Anne winks at me before turning around, preparing to toss the bouquet. She counts down from ten, and I watch as Hadley takes an athletic stance like she's prepared to draw blood for that bouquet. I chuckle to myself, loving that feisty lady even more. My Bully.

When Mary Anne gets down to three in her countdown, I quickly make my way to the mosh pit of women. It was harder than I thought to shove through, but I make it just in time to stand behind Hadley as Mary Anne says one, turns around, and walks directly to Hadley, placing the bouquet into her surprised hands.

"Turn around," Mary Anne says through her wide smile.

Hadley turns around, and comes face to face with me.

"What's going on?" she asks, her blue eyes dancing like light reflecting off the ocean. "Are you proposing again?"

I laugh at her bluntness, but shake my head.

"Now that would be too cheesy." I smirk, putting one palm face up in the air and the other hand in the rock position on top of it. "Here's the deal. If I win this fight, Braxton's Day is still on, and I can cash it in whenever I please. If you win, I give up my day to you. Deal?"

She eyes me warily, probably wondering what the heck has gotten into me to stop wedding festivities like this. Little does she know how I'm fixing to change her life as she knows it with my earned day from watching *Twilight* with her.

Yes, I plan to win this fight.

And I plan to cash in on my day as soon as we get back to Mississippi.

"Fine. Let's fight." Her hands mirror my own, except her right still sports the black brace. She doesn't make full contact with that hand.

"Rock, paper, scissors, shoot!" we yell in unison. Our words echo around the ballroom. She pulls scissors, as is typical of her first round, and I pull paper.

"You aren't here to play, Rawls," she comments at my lack of pulling rock, a smile tugging at the corner of her lips.

"I'm here to win." I wink.

"Rock, paper, scissors, shoot!" She pulls paper, and I pull rock. I stuck with the usual flow while she changed her game up.

"Match point," I whisper, my voice low and husky. I can't wait to win this.

We're preparing for the final round when Hadley's phone rings. The ballroom had become so quiet that the soft volume of her phone seems to surround us. She groans and slips the phone from her pocket and answers the call.

Wait, that dress has pockets?

"Kind of in the middle of something," she barks at the person on the other end of the line. I watch as her face transforms from irritation, to shock, to panic. "Okay, I'll see how fast I can make it back." She clicks the phone off.

Clearing her throat, she glances at all the faces watching us. Some are people we know from back home and others are perfect strangers. She turns to Mary Anne, whispers something in her ear, then gives her a tight hug.

"Go," Mary Anne says. "Text me with an update when you can."

With that, Hadley grabs my hand and pulls me out of the ballroom.

Chapter Twenty-Eight

HADLEY

W hy, *why*, did I not tell Braxton about Mama earlier? If I had, I wouldn't be in this stupid, sour pickle. I let out a breath, then two. He's going to hate me...

"I need a HUGE favor," I begin, still catching my breath from bolting out of the wedding reception, Braxton in tow. I release his hands and take a step back, staring down at my black toeless heels. Braxton doesn't respond, so I continue. "That was Lorelei. Mama is in the hospital. She apparently took some drug from an inmate, and now she is unconscious and fighting for her life."

"Inmate? Was she back in prison?" Braxton finally speaks up. I simply nod, still refusing to meet his gaze. He clears his throat before speaking again. "How long has she been there?"

Here goes the conversation I was so desperately trying to avoid the same way I dodge chicken on bread. "She was arrested the day before we left. I didn't want to deal with it and figured she could wait until we got home for me to bail her out...again." I should use this red color on my nails more often. It matches my favorite lipstick perfectly.

"Hadley." Just the way he says my name has guilt burrowing into my stomach like carpenter bees creating holes for their eggs in the wooden poles of my porch back home. "Why didn't you tell me sooner? We could have worked something out. You know Brandi could have—"

"That's exactly why I didn't tell you," I interrupt, finally dragging my eyes up to his. I can't take his sorrowful, let-me-help-you tone. "You are always trying to help. Trying to butt up in my business. Mama is *my* business, not yours." Why can't he see that? Braxton doesn't deserve to have to deal with my issues. His sympathy only makes me feel inferior to him and his perfect family and perfect life.

He stares at me, blinking once, then twice, as if he can't believe the words I'm saying right now. But I can't seem to stop.

"I've got to go home and take care of this. Whether I agree with Mama or not, she is my only living relative that I know. Unlike you, I don't have the perfect mother, or father, or a sibling. I don't have anyone, for that matter, who carries my same blood and DNA that would give a rat's booty about me." At my words, the giant of a man before me seems to grow small. His green eyes shine bright through a veil of water as he runs a hand through perfectly gelled and tousled onyx hair.

"Okay," he says in barely a whisper. "Let's go grab our things then."

More guilt gnaws at me. "I'm flying back home. I need to get there as fast as possible. Just in case she…" I trail off, not able to finish that sentence. I love my mama, no matter her sins and wrongdoings. She's my only blood, besides Grandmama, who has loved me. A twisted, selfish love, yes. But nonetheless, she's all I have.

"And you need me to drive you to the airport, then drive the truck and our stuff home." He finishes describing my unasked favor that I need.

"I'll take a rideshare to the airport. I'm sorry. Please, I've got to go." I soften my voice, the pain I've caused him clear as day on his handsome face. But that's what I do. I self-destruct. And Braxton needs—deserves—so much better. He nods, and I take a step closer to him and tilt my head up, hoping for one last kiss before the inevitable. He turns his head away at my attempt, and I shrink down to the size of an ant.

Without another look, I turn on my heel and make a beeline for my room while ordering the soonest plane ticket home. Thankfully, there is a plane with an extra seat leaving for Jackson, Mississippi, in two hours with only a thirty-three minute layover in Atlanta for a connecting flight. I buy the last ticket, once again thankful that I had saved a decent nest egg and was conservative with my spending habits after college.

I make it to my room, becoming a raging storm the way I move about it, picking up my messiness and throwing things into my suitcase and other bags at random. I pack my laptop backpack with necessities for travel; I'll leave the rest for Braxton in his room.

Only moments later, I have my bags packed, sweatpants and Braxton's black t-shirt that I stole yesterday on, and running shoes laced on my feet. I open the door to leave the hotel room and run smack into Braxton's chest, dropping the luggage I was planning to bring to his room and shoving my braced wrist against his rock hard abs. *Holy ouch.*

"You're not getting a rideshare. I'm taking you to the airport." His voice is monotone and his expression glazed over.

"You don't have to—"

"Stop talking," he says in that same, formal voice. "You can take the plane home by yourself. I'll drive myself back home. But I'm taking you to the airport."

I don't have time to fight him, plus the nearest rideshare is twenty minutes away.

"Let's just go," I say, picking up my dropped luggage and shoving ahead of him. He trails directly behind me, not bothering to match my pace like he usually does. I can't help but feel that it's purposeful. His legs are much longer than mine, afte rall.

We make it to his truck and take the silent, short drive to the Norfolk airport.

One thing is very clear as I make my way to TSA and Braxton walks away from me without watching me go through the line: I've lost my new boyfriend.

More importantly, I've lost my best friend.

The flight went smoothly, thank the universe. Or whatever I'm supposed to thank. It's hard to know in circumstances like these. I thought for a moment I'd acknowledged God's existence. Up on those slopes, it seemed impossible to deny Him. When Braxton sings to Him, I know he's not feigning the emotion written across his closed eyes and reverent expression. I started to believe...just maybe...

Then the other shoe dropped.

"Oh good, you made it!" I hear Lucy's voice before I see her. I whip around to find her sitting near baggage claim. Thankfully, I don't have to wait.

"Let's go," I say.

"Lorelei is at the hospital. Rose Lynn is stable, but still unconscious." Lucy continues to update me as we make it to her car parked in the airport garage and begin the three hour drive back to Juniper Grove. Honestly, flying home only saved me about three hours. I guess a little more if you include any stops we would have had to make while driving straight through.

Lucy tells me that Mama took a drug that an inmate had smuggled in somehow, according to the guard on duty (who I will definitely be hunting down and having a chat with). Then Mama began to complain of stomach aches and dizziness. Only minutes later, Mama erupted into full blown seizures before passing out. Her breathing and heart rate slowed to dangerous levels before stopping all together. The doctors were able to revive her, but she's still unconscious.

"I should have bailed her out before leaving on that stupid road trip," I state, gazing out the window as we pass by a wall of green.

"Don't be so hard on yourself, Hads. You didn't know this would happen. You are not her keeper."

"But I am. Who else does she have?" I ask. I'm not mad at Lucy for her statement, but I wish she understood. Why would a statement like that from Braxton light my fire, but from Lucy, it's taken as support? I guess with him, there's too much envy for his perfect life.

And in that moment, I realize I forgot one important, recent detail of Braxton's life. He lost his sweet, kind mama to cancer as she wasted away in a hospital bed.

The guilt I experienced earlier in his presence is nothing compared to the utterly disgusting sickness washing over me in waves. I am a truly terrible person for lashing out at him like that. Especially when his perfect life was shaken so hard last year at the loss of his mama. Hearing my mama was in the hospital probably stirred up unwelcome memories. Why couldn't I have thought about all that during the moment? It sure would have saved me from making a total snake of myself.

"Maybe this will be a wakeup call for her. Maybe this time she'll get her life right." Lucy's words jolt me from my thoughts. I can only hope it will be a wakeup call for Mama.

Maybe I need a wakeup call, too. No, I'm not an addict like Mama, but I share her tenacious, selfish attitude.

And that has got to *change.*

CHAPTER TWENTY-NINE

BRAXTON

The rumbling of the tires hitting the grooves in the side of the road makes my eyes snap open. *Shoot.* I need to find a gas station, stat. Checking the time on the dash, I sigh. Only four more hours of driving.

After dropping Hadley off at the airport, I went back to the hotel and packed my own bags. I told Mary Anne and David congratulations again, informed them of Hadley's travel plan, and left. My brain has been in a constant fog since she snapped at me.

"Unlike you, I don't have the perfect mother, or father, or a sibling."

Her words penetrate the fog inhabiting my head every now then, sending strikes of agony through my soul.

Mom died in a hospital bed. In the same hospital Rose Lynn is probably in right now. Though it's been a little over a year since her death, it's still fresh on my mind like it happened yesterday. The pain I feel associated with those memories still sting like the moment she closed her eyes. I know she's in a better place, a much happier place, with our Savior. But dang, it still hurts like heck.

I don't think Hadley was aware of what she was saying at that moment. Anger, frustration, and sadness had consumed her. The light blue eyes I love so much had darkened like a tropical storm brewing over the Gulf of Mexico. She didn't mean to stab me with her words, I have to believe that. But I'm kind of glad she took a plane and is not sitting in my passenger seat right now. I need the space.

A light flickers ahead, and I pray it's a gas station. Praise be, it is! I pull in, stretch my legs, and buy one of those new, supposedly healthy, energy drinks. I try to avoid them, but this drive requires one, much like drives from the Gulf up to Juniper Grove when I get off the rig. My phone rings, and it's Michael. Why's he calling me in the middle of the night? *God, Brandi better be okay.* I can't take anything else…

"Michael, what's wrong?" I answer, my mind already hurtling to worst case scenarios. Man, I need sleep.

"Everything's fine," he says gently. I assume he hears the tired panic in my voice. "I heard earlier from Brandi that Hadley's mom was in the hospital and that she'd flown home. I figured you were on the road."

How does news travel so fast in that small town? My sister had texted me to be safe driving home and that she was going to look into what happened at the jail and why. For once, I'm thankful Brandi is an attorney and pries into other people's business.

And that's exactly what Hadley accused me of doing. Maybe it just runs in the family. But is it really such a bad thing when you're doing it because you genuinely love and care about protecting someone? I get that Hadley is independent. I get that she hasn't had the best upbringing and has had to do so many things by herself with only her disabled Grandmama in her corner. But I'm in her corner. Can't she see that?

No one should have to do life all alone.

"Stopped for a minute to stretch my legs," I reply to Michael after he clears his throat, bringing my attention back to him.

"How much longer until you make it back?"

"A little under four hours now. Hopefully I won't have to stop again after this one." I decide to go ahead and fill up the tank though the gas price here is probably forty cents higher than that of one I'd find in the next city.

"I've got a proposition for you," Michael says.

"Mhmm," I mumble before taking a sip of the drink. I almost spit it out because it definitely doesn't taste like the cotton candy flavor it claims to be. Setting it inside the truck, I pay for gas then get to pumping.

"My company landed a huge contract on a vacation home for Mason Kane. Do you know who that is?" Despite my current broody mood, I laugh.

"Yeah, I know him."

"I thought so because he has one stipulation."

Not too weird for a star, I guess. "What's th—?"

Michael begins before I even finish the question. "He wants you to design it. Now obviously since you aren't licensed, our current architect will have to—"

I hear Michael continuing to talk in the background, but I'm not processing his words. Mason Kane wants *me* to design his vacation home? I showed him a few pictures of houses I either designed or helped Mom design while Mason and I worked out in a hotel gym bonding over the friend zone.

It's almost as if I can hear God saying, "My plans always work out in My timing."

"Whoa," is the only word that I can manage to get out.

"So, will you do it?"

Will I? Designing, becoming an architect, was the dream. But when Mom got sick, and I needed to step up, I did. The medical bills are mostly paid off now, and I could afford a career shift. Is it too late in life though?

"Not to pressure you or anything," Michael laughs, "but I could genuinely use this contract."

I weigh the idea. I would need to go back to school to get licensed, but I do have a few classes under my belt from the beginning of college. I think it would make Mom happy if she was here. Plus, I'm sick of leaving Hadley for a month at a time. Even when we were just friends, I hated leaving her.

Are we still a couple?

Ha, who am I kidding? No matter the hurtful words, I love that woman more than anything. She's not going to self-destruct herself out of my life that easily. She threw on *my* shirt to travel in. There's no way I'm letting her go without giving it my best fight. She's going to stop self-sabotaging herself, or she's going to really miss me by the time this is over.

And this career shift just might help me out in that department.

"I'm in."

CHAPTER THIRTY

HADLEY

B *eep. Beep. Beep.* The sound of the heart monitor echoes through my ears. It should provide a comforting feeling, knowing Mama's heart is working and pumping at a normal rate. But instead, each beep stirs a new level of dread within me. The fact that she's handcuffed to the bed also infuriates me.

"She's going to be okay," Lorelei whispers beside me, placing a hand on my shoulder.

"There are so many things we could do together if she would clean up her act," I vent, trying unsuccessfully to hold back tears. "We could restore our relationship. Become an actual mother and daughter combo. She could give me away at my wedding, and I could pick at her for dressing like an old woman while secretly loving her hipster fashion choices. We could have dinners around the table. Me, her, and Braxt—" I stop myself.

Braxton isn't a part of the equation anymore, and it's all my reckless and selfish temper's fault. There's no way he will accept me back after that off-hand comment about his mama and their perfect life. There was a line, and I flew past it like I was gunning for the Nascar championship title.

"What happened between you two?" Lorelei asks. Lucy, who's been texting away on her phone for the past thirty minutes, clicks it off and joins us. I hadn't told them much before getting on the plane, just that I had once again royally screwed over my own life and happiness. I tell my best friends through my tears of the comment I made, how he reacted, and all the other things. I let them know that I finally told Braxton about that night in college, and that he had accepted me and wasn't disgusted by me.

"And that's how I repay him," I scoff. "By bringing up his mama in such an awful manner in the heat of my anger."

"I'm sure he understands," Lucy says. "Braxton isn't the kind of guy to blame you for that." She's right. Maybe he would take me back and forgive me. But that's what makes it all the worse.

Braxton Rawls is too good for me. Even as a friend.

Light as a feather, Mama's finger touches the outside of my hand resting beside hers.

"Call the nurse!" I stand up, hovering over Mama for more signs of consciousness. Slower than honey dripping from a spoon, Mama opens her eyes.

Before I can say a word to her, the nurses arrive and take over, shoving me (and the chair I was sitting in) out of the way. I bring my chair to the back of the room and sit while Lucy and Lorelei stand on either side of me. Both of my friends have a hand on my shoulder from their respective sides, gluing me down to the chair.

I watch the chaos ensue as the nurses check vitals, ask her how she's feeling, write things down. A policeman stepping into the doorway captures my attention from the fluttering around Mama. Right behind him, Brandi Kelly appears. I try to stand up to go see her, but the women at my side continue to hold me down.

"Guys, it's Brandi," I state. They follow my gaze and let me up.

I step outside, side-eying the officer as I do. I'm still having mixed feelings about the law enforcement in this town for letting Mama get her hands on something that almost killed her while in prison.

Once outside, I crumble into the arms of a shocked Brandi. It's not that we don't like each other. We've always been friends, but it's rare I confide in her or melt down in front of her like this.

"Shh, it's okay," she says, sounding eerily like Braxton when he comforts me. Her hand even finds its way to the back of my head where she presses it against my scalp.

A tender show of love that her brother often shows me.

I pull away after a moment, wiping my eyes. I'm sure the makeup from the wedding is either gone by now or I look like the Joker from Batman. Funny how thoughts about how I looked never crossed my mind from the moment I went through TSA and watched Braxton walk away from me.

"Listen, I'm going to do everything I can to investigate how that inmate was able to smuggle in whatever drug that was and how your mom was able to get her hands on it," Brandi says. "I've got my paralegal working on it already."

"Thank you," is all I manage to say through my sniffles. It's nine in the morning and I'm exhausted from the lack of sleep and traveling through the night. Don't even get me started on the emotional whirlwind of the past couple of days. "Where's...did Braxton make it home?"

"About an hour ago," she says with a soft expression.

"Good. Maybe he can get some sleep." The words sound as convincing as they feel. I don't want him to get any sleep. I want him to show up here, despite everything. That's what he usually does. But then again, kissing a man and declaring your love to him changes the typical designated friend status...

"Miss Dawson?" One of the nurses motions me to come inside. I slide past the policeman again and rush to Mama's side. Her blue eyes, so similar to my own, fill with tears when she sees me. Hot tears trail down my own cheeks.

"Mama?"

"Hadley Bear," she says, using the nickname she's always called me when she was clean and in her right mind. Mama is a petite, curvy woman, much like me, but her features look sharp in comparison to her sunken cheeks. Guilt racks my consciousness once again for not bailing her out before I left.

"I'm so sorry, Mama. I should have got you out of that place." She closes her eyes and sighs.

"Can someone uncuff her hand, please?" I turn and glare at the policeman. He makes no motion toward me. "*Please,*" I nearly beg. He must take pity on me because he does as I ask. Not both hands, but the one closest to me.

I take her hand between mine.

"What happened to your hand?" Mama asks.

"I sprained it while skiing," I laugh, recalling the memory. "I bet Braxton I could *fall* better than he could." Mama tries to laugh, but it's a dry, throaty sound that turns into coughs.

"Where is he?" she asks. My heart constricts in my chest, taking my breath with it.

"He's home now." I can't tell her of our brief relationship. Nor can I bear to tell her that she probably won't see much of him around anymore. Mama and I don't spend a lot of time together as it is, so she doesn't see Braxton often. But when he is around, it's like Mama is a new person.

Braxton always treats her with respect, love and kindness. Not like the town's outcast.

I made the biggest mistake of my life pushing him away.

If he was still mine, he would have been here. Not at his house, but holding me close regardless of my inclinations to push him away.

"Hadley. I want you to know right now," Mama says as her eyes flutter in search of sleep. "It's not going to be easy. In fact, it's going to be quite difficult. But I want to be better. I'm going to be better. I'm done with drugs and alcohol. I'm going to be the mother you—" her voice drifts off as her eyes shut. I'm not naïve enough to believe her, but the words still stir a little hope. Maybe this did get her attention after all.

"It's the medicine I gave her," the nurse says beside me. "She needs to sleep while the drug continues to flush out of her system so that her heart rate doesn't destabilize again."

"Should you have given her that?" I question. Mama does have a past when it comes to narcotic addictions.

"It's a low dose and is non-addictive. She won't have any when she leaves here."

I nod and look around for Lorelei and Lucy. I find them in the hallway talking to Brandi.

"One of you take me home, please," I tell Lorelei and Lucy.

I'm so tired.

●🖐️👆

"Hadley, we're here." Lucy's voice stirs me awake. My eyes groggily open and I somehow make it out of the car and into the twins' home.

"Why are we at your house? I said to take me home."

"You need some rest, and we live closer to the hospital," Lucy replies. Lorelei's coming behind us.

"But my bed..." I yawn.

"You can use mine for now." I'm too tired to continue to argue. Lucy ushers me into her room and points to her bed. "Lay down. Rest."

I don't fight it.

The next time I open my eyes, it's to Lorelei gently shaking my shoulders while whispering for me to wake up.

"Come one, Hads. We need to get you ready."

Groaning in protest, I swat her away.

"Hadley Anne. Get up." She hits my shoulder, and I flinch away. The covers shuffle around me as I push myself into a sitting position and then rub the sleep from my eyes. What time is it?

"Alright, alright. I'm up. What am I getting ready for? And what time is it?"

"It's evening. Time for you to get up and make yourself decent. I'm taking you home shortly."

I groan again, falling back onto the bed and burying my face in a pillow. "Can't I sleep over here tonight?"

Lorelei clicks her tongue while hauling me to my feet. "For a petite woman, you are heavy in dead weight mode." I don't bother to be of assistance by holding my own weight.

"That's because I don't want to leave this bed."

"Too bad. You need to go home. Lucy and I have company tomorrow and I need to make sure this place is tidy."

I roll my eyes at her. "Since when do you kick me out for company? What's going on?"

Lorelei sighs, pulling me into the bathroom. She begins combing through my hair, and I close my eyes, enjoying the tingling feeling it gives me.

"I've just got to get you home, okay? Everything's fine. Jake is apparently coming over to talk things out with Lucy." She puts that last part in air quotes. "And I have quite a bit of work to do. So I want to go ahead and make sure you get home safely."

"Hmm, okay," I say. "But why do I have to get decent? Trust me, I'm going straight to bed when I get home."

The corner of Lorelei's lips twitch upward. "I bet you will. You've had a long day."

"The longest," I reply. "Um, Lor? What do I need to do for Braxton? I've got to find a way to apologize and show him just how sorry I am. Even if we can't be—" I choke on the next word, "together, I need him in my life as a friend. I can't lose him, Lor. I can't—" I begin sobbing through labored breaths.

Lorelei runs her fingers through my now smooth hair. "Tell him that. Be honest with him."

"Is that enough? I feel like I need to make a grand gesture or something."

She smiles softly and meets my eyes through the bathroom mirror. "You've always been enough for that man."

My heart thumps, thumps, thumps right out of my chest.

"I hope you're right, Lor. When are you going to find yourself a man?"

She scoffs. "Like I have time for that. You know I'm not a romantic."

"So? That doesn't mean you can't have love."

Her phone buzzes, then she shoots a text back to someone. She nods silently to herself as she slips her phone into her pocket. "Let's get you home."

CHAPTER THIRTY-ONE

BRAXTON

I wake up to the sun setting, kicking myself for sleeping too long. I had planned to take a short nap before going to find Hadley at the hospital. Picking up my phone, I realize why the alarm I set never woke me up—my phone died. Searching through my bags thrown haphazardly across my floor, I finally find the white charger and plug it into my phone.

What's gotten into me? I'm an organized, meticulous person...even when I'm exhausted. I'm not the person who forgets to plug in his phone. I can only blame it on things not being right with Hadley, and I need to fix that pronto.

After my phone gets juiced enough to turn on, I send a quick text to Lorelei. I trust her with my secret plan more than Lucy. Only moments later, Lorelei replies, first berating me for being so late but then telling me the plan's a go. I pat the pockets of my black suit pants (yes, I'm still in my wedding day attire), checking to make sure it's still there. The band of Mom's ring meets my finger, and I grin like a fool.

It still doesn't feel real.

I dig through my bags once more to find and slap on fresh deodorant, find my toothbrush, then head to the bathroom to brush my teeth. My heart is continuously beating like a wild race-horse, no matter how many times I scold it to calm down. Maybe it's too early? Maybe she really doesn't want me anymore after Chesapeake?

No, I don't subscribe to that. Hadley was just angry and tired and confused. She loves me, I'm sure of it. And we've been soul-mates since I was nine and she was seven. It's rare to find the one your soul longs for that young, but we did. And I'm not wasting another moment without her by my side in the eyes of the town, the law, and most importantly, God.

I finish my light grooming session before jumping back into my truck once more to drive to Hadley's house.

Gosh, I miss when we used to live only minutes apart. The drive is still a short one to her house, but it's nothing like being able to walk over whenever I wanted. We spent so much time in her current house when it was still her grandmama's. Baking, wrestling, watching movies, and staying up as late as Grandmama (she insisted I call her that too) would let us.

That's why it's the perfect spot to ask for Hadley's hand in marriage.

I pull up and snag the key from under the hide-a-key rock. I text Lorelei to let her know I'm here, and I thank her again for persuading Hadley to go to their place instead of here.

Stepping inside, I quickly get to work setting up the house like I need it. Dad calls me as I'm stuffing ammo inside the old tire swing Hadley and I used to play on.

"Hey, Dad," I answer.

"Hey, son. What's this I hear about you going back to school for your architect license and joining Michael's company?" I can hear the smile in his voice. *Guess you got your way after all, old man,* I laugh while shaking my head.

"The timing was right," I comment.

"Well, good for you. I'm proud of you."

I tighten my grip on the phone. "Now you're proud of me? Because I got a job that *you* approve of?"

Silence stretches on, and I loosen up, regretting my harsh tone. It's the lack of restful sleep.

"I'm sorry, I shouldn't have said that." I finally admit.

"It's okay, son," he says. "I've always been proud of you. You stepped up when the family needed you. I've just been thinking it's your turn to not have to make sacrifices. That's why I've been pushing you to get a different job. Offshore didn't make you happy."

An unfamiliar feeling of guilt clenches my gut.

"Dad, I—I didn't know you felt that way."

"It's alright," he says, resorting back to the man of few words I know so well. "Want to come over for dinner?"

"I'm actually in the middle of something." I pause. "I'm fixing to propose to Hadley."

"Good for you, son," he says as if he knew this would happen all along. "Do you have your mother's ring?"

I swallow. "Yes."

"Alright, well, I'll let you go. Good luck." And with that, he clicks off.

A weight lifts from my chest, one that I didn't realize was there. *Dad's always been proud of me. He just wanted me to be happy in my career.* With a new sense of determination, I work twice as fast to set up.

My heart still hasn't quit racing, and I'm kind of wondering if I should see a doctor. My hands grow clammy, which results in me dropping items like the Nerf gun and lollipops over and over again. But at last, I finish everything I needed to do, thankful that I took one last stop on my way home to get what I needed, and shoot Lorelei a text.

Me: Bring the woman over. I'm ready.

Lorelei and Lucy live a little further away from Hadley than I do, so the staring at the clock thing I've been doing makes the minutes drag on slower than I think is scientifically possible. It's during this time that doubt creeps in.

Not for one second do I doubt that Hadley and I belong together, but I do doubt the eventual workings of our future. What if she never surrenders to Jesus like me? Will she want to keep our kids from church? Is the fact that she's not a Christian going to cause a lot of disunity? Every question is valid, and I know exactly what everyone says: "Do not be unequally yoked." It's in Scripture for a reason. I don't know how to reconcile that verse with my love for Hadley.

She's kind, considerate, and full of love. She's the woman who holds the door for elderly people and will cook a meal for a sick community member. She's always serving and loving others through her career and personal life. Sure, she's made her fair share of mistakes...but who hasn't?

And maybe that's the problem...she doesn't see herself the way I see her.

The turning of the door knob brings me back to reality. The door opens, then quietly clicks shut, as if she is trying to make as little noise as possible. Her quiet footsteps tell me she's headed down the hallway.

Game on, I smirk, gripping my Nerf gun assault rifle from my position in the guest bathroom. She'll never make it back to this room in the dark.

CHAPTER THIRTY-TWO

HADLEY

I don't know what Braxton's getting at here, but he knows I can't resist a challenge. Now I see why Lucy brought me to her and Lorelei's house instead of home. And why Lorelei was so persistent in getting me home tonight. She dropped me off without so much as an explanation as to why there were lollipops sticking out of my grass, lining my walkway. The moment I was out of her car, she zoomed off with a wave. Without a doubt, this has something to do with Braxton.

When I make it to the door, I notice a note taped to it, directly at my eye level. It's in Braxton's signature scrawl, though I can tell he tried to write bigger than usual.

The note read:

Braxton's Day begins now (yes, I'm aware it's 6 pm, but I couldn't wait). Also, I'm aware we never finished fighting for it back at the wedding, but let's be honest, I would have won anyways. This

Nerf gun is yours. Others are stationed throughout the house and
backyard, along with ammo.
  May the best shot win.
  P.S. no lights allowed!!

My heart swells. If nothing else, this note and little game he
planned proves he still wants me in his life. At least as a friend. If I
can't have him as my boyfriend, then he HAS to remain my friend.
He's the very air I breathe, and it took me ruining it all to finally
figure it out. From now on, if Braxton wants to help me, I'm letting
him. He has always respected my independence, and it was foolish
of me to think he wasn't because he was looking out for my best
interest.

After tying my hair into a bun using the ponytail holder around
my wrist, I pick up the gun he left for me and turn it in my hands.
It's a little one-shot pistol style thing. I chuckle to myself. The man
isn't playing fair. He's probably got a bazooka or something in
there. Do they make bazooka Nerf weapons?

As stealthily as possible, I turn the knob to the front door and let
myself into the pitch black house. Did he really cover the windows?
I touch the fabric over the window by the door, feeling the rough
texture of black tarp. When and where did he get this from? I shake
my head, knowing this is going to end in one epic failure for me.

I close the door, quiet as a mouse, and feel my way down the
hall with my braced hand, the Nerf pistol cocked and loaded in the
other. The plan is to hide out in the guest bathroom since it is at
the far end of the house and is a prime location to make sure he
doesn't sneak up behind me.

My heart pounds in time with my footsteps as I near the bathroom. I reach out with my braced hand expecting to have to push the door open, but to my surprise, my hand falls through the air. With my pistol out, I take a step into the small room and shuffle quietly toward the shower. I lift my foot to step in, but instead of my foot landing on the other side of the tub, it lands on top of the shower curtain, and I fall straight on top of a body, taking the curtain with me.

My mind reels. I *never* close the shower curtains after a shower. When a guest is finished in this bathroom, I always make sure the curtain is open.

Why? That night in college when I was drunk and needed to use the restroom. The shower curtain was closed, as is typical in most people's homes, so when it moved while I was washing my hands, I froze.

That's when *he* reached out and...

"Hadley!" A panicked voice shouts my name, pulling me from the consuming memories. "Hadley, are you okay? Does anything hurt?" Braxton. His sweet, breathy sound wraps me in a hug, ever so gently calming my breathing. I'm home. With Braxton.

And I landed on top of him when I fell...

I try to jump up, but that's extremely hard to do when you are on top of a man in a bathtub with a thick shower curtain tangled around you.

"Uh," I scramble for words while trying to get myself out of this awkward situation.

"Hold still," he says. I feel his hands grasping at my hips and have half a mind to shove him away. The other half wants him to come closer.

"What are you doing?"

"Trying to get you off me so we can get up." He laughs—*laughs!*—at our current predicament.

"I can get myself out, thank you very—"

"Yeah, yeah. I know you can. But I like getting to do it." His hands tighten around my hips as he lifts me off him like I'm a mere child, setting me outside the shower where my legs refuse to stand. I collapse to the ground. "Good gracious, woman. Did you break your legs in that fall?"

Stupid weak knees. All he did was lift me off him by my hips and talk about how he liked it. Nothing to get all flustered over. He's had to pry me off him in the past plenty of times during our wrestling matches as kids.

And my knees worked fine then.

I lean against the wall, taking steadying breaths.

"Sorry about that," I begin. "I normally keep the shower curtains open."

He laughs. "I've noticed in the past. Should have remembered that before closing myself off in here. Why do you do that anyway? It causes mold, you know."

Now it's my turn to laugh. The memory is still there, tugging at the edges of my brain, but being with Braxton is like anchoring my soul to solid, unshaking ground.

"I don't want to go into detail, but it involved what I told you about back in Chesapeake." Silent moments pass. "But I'm okay.

Seriously. I'm not going to go into panic mode like last time. It helps with you being here..." My voice trails off at the admission.

"I'll always be here, Hadley."

Tears stream down my face. "I'm so sorry for what I said."

"It's already forgiven," he says, shattering and mending my heart at the same time somehow.

"You've known me for so long," I say. "You know my scars, nightmares, and demons. But you still love me. Why?" The words come out muffled through the tears and my hands covering my face.

"Ultimately, because God loves. I can only love people, you included, because He loves me. *He loves you.*" He emphasizes that last part.

"Then why did He give me this pathetic, crappy life?"

"Is your life really that bad, Hadley?" The question stops me in my tracks. Yes, my past really is that bad. But now? Look where I am. I have my own business and brand, best friends who love me, a man who I know would give me the world should I ask, and a mama who may or may not be getting right—the jury is still out on that one.

I swallow. "No, I guess it's not."

"You see, God doesn't promise us perfection. He promises that He'll be there with us through it all. The good. The bad. And the awful."

That's a God I would be willing to learn more about. Braxton is so sincere, and I do want to talk with him more about it later.

But that's a thought for another time.

Because I'm supposed to be in the middle of a war.

"What's with all this?" I ask, gesturing around me. Then, I remember it's pitch black and he can't see me.

My whole body flushes, heat spreading, well, everywhere. Emotions get way too intimate in the dark. I gather my strength to stand and quickly find the light switch. The illumination hurts my eyes for a moment, but then I adjust.

Braxton sits in the tub, his back opposite the faucet and knees bent toward his chest. The shower curtain lies half on him and halfway on the floor where I was. I meet his eyes and they twinkle with mischief. He reaches over the tub and grabs a Nerf gun sitting on the floor. Not a bazooka, but something much fancier than my pistol.

Where is my pistol?

I frantically search the small room, finding it in the toilet bowl.

"You closed the shower curtain, but couldn't put the toilet lid down?" I raise an eyebrow at him.

"Guess you're going fishing for it." He smirks, holding his own gun up.

"Not a chance, Rawls."

"Then I guess you're already out of the game because," his already deep voice lowers an octave, "I've got you in my sights."

With all the confidence I can muster after that incident, I saunter the few feet between the light switch and tub to stand directly in front of him. Bending down to get eye level with him and the Nerf gun he has pointed at me, I gently use my dominant hand to lower it and lean over, mere inches from Braxton's lips. The moment he closes his eyes, I snatch his weapon away from him and run.

Could I have pelted him with Nerf bullets at that moment? Sure. But where would the fun in that be?

I laugh maniacally as I run back down the hallway towards the backyard. He mentioned in the note that it was an open area for the game. Before I close the back door, I hear him growl in frustration. Then he bellows, "You better be glad I love chasing after you, Bully."

The weak knees return as I shut the back door.

No, Braxton and I aren't over. This is only the beginning.

Because I know anytime I try to run or go to a dark place, he will be there to chase me down and shower me in sunlight. That list I made detailing reasons I couldn't date my best friend?

It's torn and thrown out the window, fluttering away in the breeze.

CHAPTER THIRTY-THREE

BRAXTON

I can't even be mad at her for stealing my weapon. The anticipation of her kiss was almost better than an actual kiss. Almost.

Besides, *I* know where all the other weapons and ammo are hidden.

Snagging a Nerf rifle-style gun from inside the stove (unheated, no worries), I bust through the back door. No point in being stealthy now. I'm out for blood.

The sun has set already and the stars light up the early autumn night sky. It's actually kinda cold for a late October night in Mississippi. I scan my surroundings. Hadley's backyard isn't huge by any means, but it's big enough—and cluttered enough—for her to have squeezed into a hiding spot.

I scan the old playground equipment from our childhood, thankful she isn't on that. That old, rotten thing should be torn down and burned. I walk to the fence line, still not bothering to be quiet, and scan the trees beyond. No sight of her. I turn around, prepared to check her grandpa's old mustang parked and rusting away on the other side of the yard, but the weapon I so proudly boasted earlier is pointed at my chest.

"Check mate." Hadley smirks. I raise my weapon to meet hers.

"Then why haven't you fired?"

"I like to toy with my prey." She winks, and her finger moves toward the trigger.

Lowering my gun so I don't hit her in the face as I pull the trigger, the Nerf bullet finds its mark, hitting her stomach.

"Too bad I don't toy with mine." I laugh at her stunned expression. But that's when the real fun begins. She lets loose, Nerf bullets flying everywhere as I run away from her. She chases me, yelling "You're going to pay for that!"

A bullet hits my bottom, and I stop in my tracks and whip around. Hadley runs straight into my chest, her braced wrist slamming into my abs. I hold my arms out to steady her.

She grimaces in pain as she takes a few steps back from me.

"Hadley, are you okay? I didn't mean to..."

The woman starts laughing and peppering me with Nerf bullets again.

Until they stop coming out the barrel.

"Oh, you're done for now," I say. Tilting my head to the side and wearing a sly grin, I slowly close the distance between us. Her eyes grow wide. She drops the gun as I approach and tries to run, but I catch her around her waist and yank her against me. "Surrender."

Hadley looks up, the blonde bun sitting on top of her head smushing against my chest. She's so short I can see her full face, though it's upside down.

"Never." She tries to wiggle out of my grasp, but quite frankly, I'm not in the mood to ever let her leave my arms again. Hadley in my arms is the rightest feeling I've ever felt. A large growl erupts from her petite body. "Let me go so I can beat you!"

"Never." I repeat her word, placing a kiss on the top of her head. She finally goes still. "If I let go, promise you won't run. You know good and well there's only one way to settle this. Even though I did technically get the first hit."

"Fine. Let's fight for victory."

I let her go and she spins around to face me, hands at the ready. I match her stance. My heart races, though I don't think it's stopped beating at an abnormal speed since I began setting up earlier.

"Before we begin, I need to tell you some good news," I state. "I'm going back to school to become a licensed architect and will be working with Michael."

"Are you serious?" She breaks form, so I do too.

"Yep. No more offshore."

A smile brighter than the moon appears on her face as she says, "You don't understand how happy that makes me!"

"With that being said, let's find out who won this war." It's time. We both take our stances.

"Rock, paper, scissors, shoot!" We yell. But instead of pulling a gesture, I slide down to one knee, pulling an actual rock out of my pocket.

A diamond.

Hadley stands frozen, her hand still resting in the scissors position.

"Hadley Anne Dawson." I clear my throat, praying I don't drop my mother's ring out of my clammy hands. At her name, she drops her hands to her side. There's enough light between the stars and the light pole in the back to see tears pooling in her eyes. I fight back my own. "You're my best friend. The girl I've been choosing to spend time with since I was nine years old. Somewhere along the way, I fell deeply in love with you. God has His reasons for letting it take so long for this moment to happen, but I've always known it was you. I—"

"Braxton," Hadley whispers my name through tears. She gets on her knees and takes my hands in hers. The ring presses between our hands. I bring my other knee to the ground. "You don't want to do this."

A tinge of anger appears. "Who are you to tell me what I do and don't want?"

She cringes, and I regret my harsh tone. She speaks before I can apologize.

"I'm a basket case. I recognize my faults and know what I need to work on. But most importantly to you, I'm not a Christian." I nod, letting silence settle between us. "I care about you. An unbelievable amount, which is why I know you can't be fully happy with me until I figure out this Christianity thing."

The silence stretches on as my heart shudders over and over.

"Are you saying you want to figure it out?" I ask, still unclear what she meant by that statement. My heart's shudders turn to leaps when she nods her head yes.

"I'm not ready to commit or anything, but I do want to know more. What you said to me earlier, coupled with feelings I've been having and...the views from that snowy mountain top...He's got to exist." Tears flow freely from my eyes as I silently offer up my gratitude to Jesus. He's working, and I don't need to get in His way.

She continues. "I want to marry you. More than anything in this world. I want to wear your mother's ring proudly, but I also want to be a woman worthy of that ring."

"You are worthy of it already," I say, standing to my feet and pulling her up with me. "You don't have to say yes right now if you think that it will be too much pressure as you figure out all the things you need to. But regardless of it all," I pause to stare into her eyes, "you are worthy of this ring and so much more."

She wraps me in her arms and I pull her close.

"Yes," she whispers in my ear. The world stands still. I push her away just enough to look at her face.

"Yes? You'll marry me?"

She responds by dragging my lips down to meet hers. And after minutes of passionately kissing the woman I'm going to spend the rest of my life with, I slide my mother's ring onto her left ring finger.

"A perfect fit," she says as she admires the square diamond under the starry night. "Now let's go pick up those lollipops from the front walkway before they go bad. You've single handedly resupplied me for life, *sweetheart.*"

"Sweetheart's not bad, but it sounds too smart-alecky from your mouth."

"Sugar?"

"Old ladies call me that," I scoff. "You can do better." She raises an eyebrow, then a wicked smile crosses her face.

"Labbie," she says, matter-of-factly. "As in labrador. If I get Bully, then you get Labbie."

"No. Not in a million years. I'm fresh out of that friendly, loyal labrador zone." I take her head between my hands and show her just how out of that zone I am.

EPILOGUE

HADLEY

I'm still in the process of trying to recover from reading Braxton's written vows to me when Mama walks into the room.

"Mama, I'm so happy you're here!" I embrace her, careful not to wrinkle my dress. It's big, sparkly, and poofy. Everything I imagined I would wear if I ever got married.

Married.

My brain wanders back to his vows. I'm going to have that sheet of paper memorized before the night's through if I keep thinking about his soulful words. I'm glad we decided to exchange them on paper before the ceremony instead of in front of everyone. I didn't see him, and he didn't see me, but we stood back to back and read aloud the vows we wrote to each other.

"I'm glad they let me out of that rehab facility to witness my only daughter's wedding." Her voice is strong, nothing like the weak rasp it was while she was on drugs and drinking alcohol. She got to come home for Thanksgiving, and now she's home for my wedding. Hopefully they will let her out to celebrate Christmas, which is only two weeks away, with Braxton and me.

"Mama, will you walk me down the aisle?" I didn't ask her earlier just in case she couldn't come. She bursts into tears, nodding emphatically. This is the perfect day. We hug again before Lucy pulls me away.

"We have to watch the makeup and hair," she says, her voice too high for her own good. She may be more excited for this wedding than I am.

Ha, who am I kidding?

I've been dreaming about this day since Braxton asked me back in October. We didn't want to wait long because...well, you can guess why, but I also wanted to wait until I was sure about what I believed.

"God, thank You so much for everything," I whisper aloud, trying my hardest not to cry and ruin Lucy's masterpiece. She wouldn't let me do my own makeup even though I'm fantastic at it because "the bride shouldn't lift a finger on her wedding day."

I'm so thankful for my best friends and the work they did to make this intimate wedding happen quickly. From the flowers and minimum decorations to the seats and tables borrowed from the Juniper Grove Church, the one Braxton's dad pastors at, this wedding couldn't be more perfect. My dress was from an off-the-rack place, but it fit me perfectly and was just what I was looking for. Lorelei and Lucy held my hand every step of the way, constantly reassuring me when doubts tried to creep in.

Goodness, I'm fixing to tear up again.

"I'll never tire of hearing you talk to God," Lorelei says beside me. I knew Lucy and Lorelei were Christians too, but I didn't know they were praying for me to surrender like Braxton was. I get it now. I understand.

I'm still not perfect, and never will be, but now I have His help to fight off my demons. That crazy love Braxton talked about...I feel it now. And even when I don't feel it, I know it's there.

"You look beautiful, baby. You've never looked more radiant," Mama says. I've tried to talk to her about God and what He's done for me, but she is still skeptical. She redirects any God-related conversations like I used to do.

"Thanks, Mama." I kiss her cheek.

"It's almost time," Lorelei says. She's been keeping Lucy and me on task through the whole process.

"Lorelei. Lucy," I address each of them, taking their hands in mine. "I love you ladies more than words can say. Not as much as Braxton," they both laugh, "but y'all are a close second. You've both been there for me so many times throughout my life, and I hope to repay you both for it one day. Y'all are the *best* best friends a girl could ask for." Lucy squeals, refraining from jumping on me with a hug. Lorelei lets a small smile escape and nods her head once.

"It's time," Lorelei says, holding out my bouquet filled with pink roses and white daisies. I wipe my hands down the front of my dress before taking my bouquet from Lorelei.

"Maddie, where are you?" Lorelei calls for one of Braxton's cousin's daughters. She's seven, so she makes the perfect flower girl. I've met her several times in the past when they were visiting with

Braxton, but they live across the state line in Tennessee. Maddie, in her adorable, frilly pink dress, comes running into the room from the guest bathroom, the one where I fell on top of Braxton while we engaged in a Nerf gun war. I'm happy to report we've played a lot more since then. And I've won the majority of them.

The girls walk ahead of me, leading me out of my room as their pale pink dresses swish around them. I didn't want traditional Christmas colors even though it's two weeks from the holiday, so I stuck with pink, which is basically a very light shade of red.

We stand at the back door, waiting for the music to start. Mama comes up beside me and interlaces her arm with mine. I smile at her, then look toward my best friends in front of me. I truly am blessed.

Dolly Parton's "More Than I Can Say" begins to play as the girls open the door and part the pink curtain behind it. I catch a small glimpse of my groom and my heart sputters. Maddie starts walking down the aisle as the curtain closes.

Lucy and Lorelei give me one last smile before stepping through the curtain and walking down the aisle together. Braxton only wanted Michael as his best man, so he's already standing beside him under the pavilion. We transformed the old playground set in my backyard to a pavilion area for cookouts and things. It's also serving as the wedding altar.

Braxton is moving into this house with me. It was a big decision for him since he designed and built that log cabin by hand. But I needed to stay here because I couldn't bear to sell Grandmama's house.

However, Braxton's house was sold to someone we trust.

The music shifts to the wedding march, and I take a deep breath. I'm caught somewhere between wanting to run to him and not wanting to take a step. Mama pulls me forward, holding the curtain open for me.

I get my first full view of Braxton. He's so unbelievably handsome in his dark gray tux. Not to brag, but he's all mine. Working construction with Michael has done a number on him. He still has several years until he finishes the program at Juniper Grove University, but he has been interning under the current architect at the request of Mason Kane.

I take a step through the curtain as the people I love stand from their seated position. The peripheral vision I was using withers away as my eyes focus solely on my best friend standing too far away from me with a tauntingly wide, kissable smile. Mama's steady pace and strong hold on my arm keeps me from bolting down the aisle.

When we make it to the front and Mama gives my hand over to Braxton's, a peace unlike anything I've ever felt washes over me. His green eyes pierce my soul as Braxton's father begins the ceremony.

The words the pastor speaks run together in my mind as I stare at the handsome, loving, kind, caring, thoughtful man in front of me. *He's all mine.* I have never felt more sure about anything in my life. My past doesn't matter right now because I know Braxton accepts me for who I was and loves me all the same. All of me.

His father asks if Braxton takes me to be his wife. Short and sweet, just like we wanted. Though my heart knows his true vows.

"I always have," he whispers to me with a smolder. I want to ask everyone to go home. Then he proudly boasts the traditional two words, "I do."

"And do you take Braxton to be your husband?"

"There's never truly been anyone else," I whisper to him, trying to match his smoldering stare. It must work because he swallows. Then I throw my hands up in victory and shout, "Heck yeah, I do!"

As his father declares us man and wife, Braxton whispers in my ear, "Don't miss this time when you kiss me." I shake my head with laughter, then draw the man's lips down to meet mine in perfect harmony.

This is true happiness.

● 🤟 ✌️

"**H**ello, Wife," Braxton says as he snatches me away from dancing with his dad—my father-in-law.

"See you later, Mr. B." I break free of Braxton and wrap his dad in an all-consuming hug.

"No need for that," he huffs in typical fashion, but his arms lightly wrap around me. Then he whispers, so softly, "I'm glad you're my daughter now."

I freeze, and then squeeze him tighter. "Thank you."

Trying my hardest to hold back sobbing tears, I turn back to Braxton and lock arms with my best friend.

My lover.

My husband.

"Hello, Husband." I give him a quick peck on the lips as we begin to sway to the live acoustic guitar. Mason Kane was in town to check the progress on his vacation house, so we asked him to come to the wedding. He volunteered to play and sing acoustic versions of his songs, much to the pleasure of our family and friends. Minus Karoline, who left when he started to play about fifteen minutes ago because she said she felt sick. Maybe I should text her and make sure she's okay. It's more for my sake than hers. I do NOT want to have to take care of a sick Braxton on our honeymoon, so I need to know just how sick she is.

"Having the wedding here was such a great idea," I say as I look around at my friends and new family. I wave to Brandi and Michael who are swaying back and forth across from us on the makeshift dance floor. "Because we can kick everyone out and go ahead and get started on the honeymoon before leaving for Chesapeake tomorrow."

"Say the word and they're gone," he rasps against my ear. A nervous laugh escapes my lips.

"We're fixing to head out." Mary Anne's signature voice catches our attention. We break apart to hug her and David goodbye.

"Oh, there's one more thing I need to do before we kick everyone out." I wink at Braxton, then jet off to find my very special guest. To my surprise, he's already chatting up the woman I wanted to introduce him to.

As I walk closer to Finley Andersson, I realize it's not Lucy he's talking to, but Lorelei.

"Finley, thank you for coming. It means so much to have you here, especially after you ratted me out back at Fableland Amusement park." He chuckles, running his hand through shaggy, blonde hair. "I see you've met Lorelei Spence."

"We bumped into each other," Lorelei says with a grimace. I then notice a stain down her dress and an empty glass in her hand.

"Again, I didn't mean to, Miss Lorelei," Finley begins, but she interrupts him.

"Quit calling me miss!"

"Oh-kay." I grab Finley by the arm and drag him away. "Best to leave her be right now. There's someone else I want you to meet anyway."

I spot Lucy by the desserts and point her out to Finley.

"Ah, the other twin from the bridal party," he muses, studying her closely.

"This one is much nicer. Her name is Lucy. I think you two could hit it off, if you get what I'm saying." I nudge his arm, and he laughs.

"Very well. I'll go say hey." Finley begins to walk off, but before he does, he turns around. "And thanks for selling me Braxton's house. It's going to be nice to have a place that's permanently mine here in backwoods Mississippi to escape to when royal life gets to be too much. I'm glad to be closer to friends than in North Carolina."

"Happy to have you here."

I search for my husband, who has apparently been telling people it's time to go as I'm stopped by everyone wanting to tell me goodbye.

Finally, the house is empty, with Lucy and Lorelei the last to leave.

"We're alone," he whispers against my ear, wrapping his strong, steady arms around my waist. "And I've waited so long for this, my *goddess divine*." My hands tremble at my sides at his use of the nickname I stole from *Pride and Prejudice*...only to be used on this occasion.

"I only wore this big, white dress so you could take it off," I tease, trying to disguise my nervousness.

"So *we* can take it off," he growls, spinning me around and leading me into my home.

Our home.

When he gets to the threshold, he picks me up bridal-style and carries me over it. He sets me down on the couch and grabs his guitar, which was leaning against the wall.

"But first, I want to play a song I wrote for you." Tears well in my eyes. He looks up after fiddling with the strings. "I haven't started yet. Why are you crying?"

"Because I've never been happier than I am in this moment." Hot liquid spills over the lids of my eyes. He smiles, genuine and content, then begins strumming a sweet melody that's wild, yet centered. Full of hope, love, and years to come.

"I call it 'Be Gentle With Me'," he says before clearing his throat. Braxton's voice, rich and smooth as melted chocolate, fills our house with my new favorite song.

If you loved the story, please consider leaving a review on Amazon and/or Goodreads!

ACKNOWLEDGMENTS

If you follow me on Instagram, then you know how excited I've been to release this book. I started writing TDF back in December of 2021 while my first book was in developmental edits. I should have been writing book two to The Politics Of... series, but this sweet story gripped my heart and wouldn't let go. Hadley and Braxton demanded to be written. I obliged.

Thank you to my Lord and Savior Jesus Christ for the gift of writing. It took me a while to finally say "yes" to the call, but now I can't imagine doing anything else. I love teaching, but writing is my heart. *Soli Deo Gloria.*

To my family—Mama, Dad, Turan, Jace, and Grandma—thanks for always cheering me on and supporting me. My sweet besties—Kaitlyn, Aubrey, and Whitney. I love you ladies so much! You three have carried me through so much the past five years. This book is dedicated to you.

To all my IG/Bookish friends...y'all are the literal best. The #bookstagram community is a light in a dark world. I'm so thankful for all the new author friends I have because of that platform. You guys rock!

Thank you to my critique partners—Devin, Latisha, and Leah. Your input, suggestions, comments, and critiques (duh) helped me out so much through this book. Lindsay, thank you for proofing this book! I love how you elevate my voice instead of smothering it. Callie, thanks for the awesome character/truck art and being such a great friend to me. Abby, I recently met you, but you are quickly becoming an important person in my life. Thanks for naming this series! People aren't wrong when they say it takes a village. So, thank you all for being a part of my village :)

To my launch team, betas, and arc readers... THANK YOU. I could not be an indie author without your constant love, support, and excitement! You keep me going. To my readers... What more can I say? I sure can't say thank you enough. A writer is nothing without a reader. You are the lifeline of this career. This book belongs to you now.

ALSO BY

Drew Taylor

The Politics of... series (sweet romance)

The Politics of Christmas (#1)

The Politics of Love (#2)

Designated series (sweet romantic comedy)

The Designated Friend (#1)

The Designated Valentine (#2)

The Designated Twin (#3)

The Designated Date (#4)

Standalones (sweet romantic comedy)

Emma Jane's Guide to Matchmaking the Mayor (**Love on the Ballot,** **#4**) → **Coming November 2024**

About the Author

Drew is on a personal mission to bridge the gap between "Christian" media and "Secular" media. She believes objects and concepts cannot be Christian, only people can be. She loves to tell engaging and sizzling romantic stories that are wrapped in reality, humor, and wit without the open doors or on-page cursing.

***

Drew is from south Mississippi but now resides in Alaska where she attempts to engage 15 and 16 year olds in classic world literature. When not teaching or writing, she enjoys reading, Bookstagram, baking Christmas goodies (even in the middle of June), researching random history facts, watching K-dramas, and spending quality time with the people who mean the most to her. Sign up for her newsletter for important updates in case Social Media decides to kick her off one day: https://mailchi.mp/61fed5b940fb/drew-taylor-author

Follow Drew:

Instagram: @authordrewtaylor

Facebook: Drew Taylor, Author

TikTok: @faithfilledromance

Pinterest: @authordrewtaylor

Printed in Great Britain
by Amazon